Love.com

Presented by
Teresa Alessi & Therone Shellman

ISBN 10: 0-9771004-4-8
ISBN 13: 9780977100446

www.thirdeyepublishing.org
www.myspace.com/theroneshellman

Third Eye Publishing, Inc.
P.O. Box 5694, Bay Shore, N.Y. 11706
(516)232-0202

Printed in the United States of America
10 9 8 7 6 5 4 3 2 1

PUBLISHER'S NOTE:
This book is a work of fiction.
Names, characters, businesses, organizations, places,
events and incidents are the product of the author's imagination or
are used fictionally.
Any resemblance of actual persons, living or dead, events, or locales
is entirely coincidental.

Cover Design/Graphics: www.mariondesigns.com
Editor: www.hightowereditorialservices.com

Acknowledgements

Most importantly we would like to thank God for allowing us to meet and present this work before him and humanity. Then we would like to thank our family and friends for the love and support.

Last but not least we would like to thank one another for taking the steps to meet one another and then following through with the completion of "Love.com."

Dedication

This book we would like to dedicate to those who dare to love even in the face of abuse and ridicule. These are the people who show and prove that love is the most powerful emotion, weapon and tool given to man by our creator. It is in love that we come to realize that it is in the nature of all things to work and come together for a greater purpose.

Chapter One

HAROLD HAS WORKED for King Drugs for ten years. King Drugs is an enormous company that delivers prescriptions to thousands of drug stores throughout the U.S. They also distribute other health care needs such as hospital beds and medical facility equipment. Harold is in charge of inventory and he knows his job in and out. Not to mention he makes pretty good money. He sits in a tiny cubicle with no windows around him and rarely goes outside of his work area during his shift. Even so, he could go anywhere within the same industry and get a managerial job making a whole lot more. His life is practical because like so many other people he fears change. Harold Fenly is a thirty-five year old, tall, thin, quiet man who has been married about eight years to his wife Linda. He's an average looking guy, but he has a stable job, a good personality and he is loyal to his friends and family.

One day after work he waved good-bye to his co-workers headed to his Jeep Cherokee Laredo and drove home listening to oldies from the sixties and seventies on his favorite radio station.

As he entered the small one bedroom apartment he shares with his wife he couldn't help but shake his head. The apartment stayed a mess because Linda kept the place cluttered with clothes, shoes and other junk. It was a horrible sight and smelled musty all the time.

Harold tried cleaning up a bit. While he was vacuuming the phone rang and when he tried to run to it, he clumsily tripped over a pair of shoes lying in the middle of the living room before tumbling to the carpet after losing his balance.

Harold was very clumsy and every time he was around something got spilled or broken. It was nothing for him to be sweeping the floor, and somehow manage to fling the broom into a picture on the wall or up into the ceiling near a chandelier. Linda always joked with him mentioning he must of broke a mirror and received seven years of bad luck.

"Hello," Harold answered, slowly lifting himself up off the floor.

"It's me," Linda snapped. "What happened what was that noise Harold? What did you do now?"

Linda is a thin, very high-spirited woman. The complete opposite of Harold. At one point she was quiet and sweet, however as years went by she grew tired of her life and upon starting her new job, Linda opened up becoming wild and outgoing. She colored her hair blond and lost weight transforming herself into a sexy woman.

Harold loved her dearly and even though she was nasty to him he worshiped the ground she walked on. While she could care less whether he lived or died. She was tired of him in every way imaginable. She was especially tired of the sex, which lasted for about 2 minutes whenever she did feel like giving in.

She ached and longed for the day when she could finally let her hair down and be free to do as she pleased.

Linda worked in a car dealership as a secretary and it was because of the job that she became flirtatious. She loved the attention she received from the male customers as well as her male coworkers. It made her hot to think about the way customers would look down her blouse or shirt whenever she wore a top revealing her breasts. She would catch them stealing a peak and she would smile to herself. Sometimes they'd be with their wives and they would become completely jealous at the way their husbands stared.

"Nothing, I am okay," he replied.

"I called to tell you I'm working late and I won't be home for dinner. There are leftovers in the fridge."

Linda controlled Harold's every action and without question, like a robot he obeyed all her wishes even though he wanted to step up at times and take control. He really wanted to put his foot down this time and tell her to bring her ass home, but he couldn't find the courage.

"Again?" he protested. "You've been working late all week you need some rest try to take off next week you deserve it."

"Yeah thanks. Who are you my boss? Good-bye Harold and don't wait up for me," she quipped.

Harold hung up and searched the fridge for leftovers. He grabbed some cold cuts and made himself a sandwich and ate it like it was the last meal he was ever going to eat. He even managed to bite the plate as he licked the remaining morsels from it.

After finishing he yawned, walked to his room and threw himself upon the bed without undressing, not even taking off his shoes.

"Man, I need to really put her in her place one of these days. Who the hell does she think she is?" He thought as he dozed off to sleep.

Linda arrived home very late that night. She tipped toed around the house as she giggled, intoxicated from the five Bahama-Mammas she had ingested. Harold was still asleep on the bed. He was snoring and wheezing like a pig and Linda was so exhausted and drunk that she threw herself on the sofa; falling asleep with all her clothes.

Chapter Two

THE NEXT MORNING after eating the eggs and toast Linda left him, Harold rushed out the door. Linda was already gone and he had overslept and didn't want to be late.

At work Harold sat in his cubicle staring at the computer as he performed his usual check up making sure the shipments arrived as requested. It was hard for him to concentrate because Linda was on his mind. First she comes home late, and then she was gone before he could get up and shower.

After awhile he felt something tickle the back of his neck and for a minute he sat there swatting at his neck trying to get rid of what ever was bothering him. His two co-workers Mark and David loved playing pranks on him. At least once a day they would scare him with something just to see his reaction. The two had tied a plastic spider to a string and they stood behind his wall, flung the spider over sliding it down his neck. After several swats at his neck Harold finally turned around and when he saw the black spider in front of him he jumped on his desk tripping over his chair before falling onto the floor.

Mark and David couldn't control themselves as they erupted with laughter. Harold tried to pick himself up however he was now tangled in the wires of the computer.

Still laughing they helped him up to get his computer and papers back on his desk.

"Thanks guys that was real mature," Harold said sarcastically.

"Come on man we're just playing," Mark said, still laughing.

Mark and Harold have been friends since high school. Harold in fact helped Mark get the gig at King Drugs. Mark worked so he could have money to play around with the ladies. Every weekend he met a different woman. Harold was different he enjoyed being married He was faithful to his wife and never went out with Mark. Linda on the other hand was out partying every night and lied to Harold that she worked late. Harold was naïve he was honest all the time. Mark wanted to wake his best friend up to face reality about the world that sometimes people are cruel.

"Tonight we're going to have a drink to celebrate David's birthday. Are you coming?" Mark asked.

"No I do not like those places," Harold mumbled as he shuffled his paperwork. "You know I hate bars. I am happily married I don't need to go out."

"Well no one said you have to hook up with anybody," Mark sneered.

"Unless you want to," David added giving Mark a pound.

"We won't tell." Mark laughed.

"We're not in high school. Y'all need to grow up you two need to find some nice woman and get married. You'll feel much better trust me." Harold turned his head so they wouldn't see the sadness wash over his face.

"I do not think so," Mark chuckled. "I bet I get laid more than you."

"OOOOH shit!" David laughed.

Harold got up and made his way toward the coffee machine trying to ignore his two friends who followed him. At that moment he realized just how long it had been since he had been intimate with Linda. He became so lost in thought that he burned his hand as his coffee cup spilled over the rim causing him to drop the mug spilling coffee all over the rug and almost splashing onto him. They all hurried away from the machine before anyone saw them.

That evening when Harold got home, he opened the door to his apartment and Linda was standing in front of a mirror wearing a short tight strapless black dress. Her breasts strained against the material as if they were trying to jump out and be seen. Harold stood amazed as he analyzed his beautiful wife instantly becoming aroused by her sexy attire. He stood there for a second, admiring her newly fit frame and quickly began imagining peeling her out of her dress.

Linda barely acknowledged him when he came in the room; she continued fussing with her appearance as she spoke to him.

"Great I am glad your home," she said.

"Are we going out?" he asked, moving towards her.

"I have a meeting," she lied. "I thought I told you about it."

"No, you didn't," he said, adjusting the bulge in his pants.

"Can you zip up my dress?" she asked, adding to his frustration.

He answered through clenched teeth. "No problem."

He helped her zip up her dress and thought about smacking her on the butt but didn't. She gave herself one last look in the mirror before kissing Harold and disappearing out the door.

After Linda left he cleaned up and decided to meet Mark at his favorite pub. Harold hadn't been to one in years but he wasn't in the mood for another night home alone.

As he entered he saw Mark was sitting at the bar with David along with several other people laughing and having a good time. When Mark noticed Harold he stood up and waved him in their direction.

"I can't believe you actually showed," Mark laughed as he pushed one guy off his stool and made Harold sit down.

"Linda had a business meeting and I had nothing better to do," Harold said sadly.

"Again Harold? First she works late then she has meetings and at night. Something ain't right."

"She has to do her job," Harold countered.

David laughed. "Man, she's a secretary!"

Mark protested to his friend as he ordered a beer. "Man wake up get more involved, your wife she doesn't sound right. Every time I see her she's dressed like she is going to a club. She never used to dress like that. I remember when y'all first met she was always home and couldn't wait to see you. Now I hardly ever see you two together. It's like she doesn't want to be around you."

"Linda is a great woman," Harold insisted. "She would never lie to me. She is very dedicated to her job. She's an important part in that dealership."

"Yeah important to her boss," Mark said making perverted gestures behind Harold's head causing everyone to bust out laughing.

"Here drink," Mark handed Harold the beer bottle. "Forget Linda and have your own fun."

Harold felt out of place. He sat there disoriented as the rest of the fellows joked and laughed.

All he could think about was Linda.

It was two o'clock in the morning and Harold had developed a headache from the combination of the music and his drunken friends. David was drunk and soaking wet from the beer that was poured on him strictly for amusement. He started kicking his feet doing some dance and accidentally kicked Harold in the leg causing Harold to fall off his stool screaming in pain. Mark was cracking up as he helped Harold get up on his feet.

"That's it! I'm going home," Harold asserted.

Mark's laughter stopped as he looked across the room and saw Linda walking in with another man who had his arm around her waist. Mark tried to distract Harold's attention away from the disaster waiting to happen but it was too late. As Harold lifted his head, he saw her and his body stiffened. The pain in his leg quickly moved to his heart. He walked toward her and her companion, never taking his eyes off of either of them.

Mark tried to stop him but he just pushed him away and continued toward her.

Harold stood in front of Linda looking at her as if she was a stranger.

"Oh my goodness!" she stuttered. "What are you doing here?"

"Guess this is a casual meeting?" he asked.

"I-uh, I-," she stammered.

Harold wasn't even angry. He was filled with regret if anything. He had actually trusted her. If he had the courage he would have reached out and smacked her.

"Harold, I can explain," Linda insisted.

Mark walked over and gave Linda a disgusted look before leading Harold out of the bar.

Harold shook his head. "She wasn't in a meeting."

"Maybe they decided to have a drink after," Mark said, trying to calm his friend.

"I can't believe how stupid I am." Harold's eyes began to tear.

Mark hugged his pal "You are not stupid you are a good man," Mark said hugging Harold.

Linda came rushing out of the bar after him.

"Listen to me Harold," she begged.

Harold stopped but did not turn to face her.

She stepped in front of him. "Please hear me out I was going to tell you. I did not want you to find out this way."

"Find out what Linda?"

Linda dropped her eyes to the pavement and spoke, "I don't want to be with you anymore Harold. I have been feeling this way for a while now."

"Excuse me? You don't want to be with me anymore?"

She finally raised her head and matched his glare. "I'm sorry."

"This is bullshit!" He began yelling loudly in the streets like a mad man.

Linda scanned the quickly forming crowd as Harold continued to rant.

"My wife is leaving me do you know that?" he screamed in a woman's face as she walked past with her husband. The woman pulled back in fear. "Watch your wife she is a bitch," he said to the man as he opened his eyes wide like a lunatic.

The man punched Harold in the face and went to grab at him but his wife pulled him away. Harold fell to the ground and Mark ran over to help him as the woman pulled her husband away.

Linda bent down to help him up.

"Get your dirty hands off me," Harold growled at her. "Get out of my sight you slut," he sneered, blood and saliva foamed around his lips.

Mark grabbed him up and pulled him toward his jeep.

Harold sat in his vehicle with Mark sitting on the passenger side.

"I am sorry Harold," Mark sighed.

"It is not your fault. It's mine she has been doing this for a while. Every night she had a new excuse not to be home and I never said anything."

"I don't get it," Mark continued. "How could she?"

"This is what I get for being me, Harold the nice guy." He punched the steering wheel. "I was always the good one. The good child, the good student, the good employee and now the asshole husband."

"Don't be so hard on yourself. You'll find some one else who will appreciate you. Linda is crazy for letting you go."

Harold looked toward Mark. "Thanks for trying to help me I'll be okay."

"Are you sure?"

Harold nodded. "Yeah, I'm good."

"Alright, I'm going to head back inside and check on David."

After his friend got out, Harold backed the truck up put it in drive and sped off.

Chapter Three

THE NEXT DAY Harold was too depressed to go to work so he disconnected his phone and sulked around his apartment all day. Later in the afternoon, Linda showed up and threw all her clothes in suitcases. He watched her move around the apartment gathering her things like she had just been paroled. Part of him wanted to beg her to stay, but a bigger part of him wanted to slap her down. Once she successfully amputated herself from his life, she left without saying a word.

Harold was just about to fix himself a sandwich when there was a knock on the door. He hesitated before answering because he really wasn't in the mood for company. But whoever it was wouldn't stop pounding, so he didn't have a choice.

"What are you doing? Why weren't you at work today?" Mark asked when he opened the door.

"She left, she came in took her clothes and left for good." Harold whined.

"Damn man, I'm sorry."

Harold collapsed on the couch crying uncontrollably. "What am I going to do now?"

"It is over! Move on like she did. What are you crying for? You need to be partying. So many men wait for this opportunity. Go and find you a new piece."

Harold shook his head. "Not me. I don't know how to be alone, and living the single life is crazy. I actually liked having someone to come home to every night."

"What are you talking about she was never home," Mark chuckled.

"Maybe I should call her. She could just be going through a phase."

"This ain't a phase Harold. She moved out!"

"I know, but I could've been there for her more," Harold groaned.

"You were always there for her. If she cared about you she would be home with you. Instead she's out with the next cat giving him the goods. You're lucky she didn't give you an STD."

Harold reached for the phone and Mark grabbed it first, tossing it to the other couch.

"Snap out of it!" Mark scolded. "She don't love you so please don't make a fool of yourself by thinking maybe they decided to have a drink after," Mark said, trying to calm his friend.

"What you're missing out on right now is old memories from years ago when she *was* a good woman to you. Think about how much of a bitch she's been lately and you'll get over her real quick."

Harold sunk back into the couch. "What am I going to do?"

Mark stood up and moved around the small space. "Harold I knew about Linda's affair for a long time now. I saw her a couple of months ago with that guy. I just didn't have the heart to tell you."

Harold's world stopped spinning and all the air was sucked out of his lungs as he stood up to face his friend.

"You saw her before?" he questioned. "What are you talking about?"

Mark let out a sigh. "Six months ago I was having some drinks when she walked in there with him. I didn't tell you because I thought he was just a co-worker or something."

"This is unbelievable!"

"I swear I didn't want to hurt you. I know how vulnerable you are. Plus you would have claimed I was lying because of how I felt about Linda." Mark said moving away from his friend.

"Get out of my house," Harold demanded.

"Okay, now you're overreacting," Mark, said moving around the couch.

"At this point I can't trust any one; all of you have been laughing at me getting your cheap thrills."

"No! No! Man I swear I didn't want to hurt you, that's it. You have to believe me."

"Just go."

Mark stood there for a second, staring at his friend. Harold knew deep down inside that none of this was

Mark's fault, but he needed someone to blame and right now there was no one around but him.

"I'll call you later," Mark said, closing the door behind him.

The next day Harold returned to work ignoring every one around him.

Mark tried getting his attention by throwing paper airplanes at him but Harold swatted them to the side. He stared at his computer trying to focus through his frustration and keep track of inventory. He got an email alert from a site called: LOVE.COM. He clicked open the email and it read: LOVE.COM is the answer to find true love. LOVE.COM will find you the ONE.

Harold got up and walked to the soda machine. He put in some change and waited for the can to come out. The can was stuck so he began to shake it then the machine started to tip over. Harold struggled to hold it up until two men who were walking in the hallway helped him out.

Back in the office he walked to the window and peaked outside suddenly becoming aware that he needed a new view on life. Like a new man he marched into his supervisor's office giving him one-week notice.

Jeremy his supervisor was displeased. "But I really count on you. Maybe we can work something out," Jeremy said.

Why do you want to go?" Jeremy asked.

"I need a fresh start somewhere else. I am tired of being shut out. I have been shut out of everything for a long time I need space."

"Is this because of what happened with your wife?"

"Yeah, laugh it up. I know I'm the talk of the office."

"No man I feel for you. I'll let you in on a secret," Jeremy said, lowering his voice. "My wife fucked my best friend."

"What did you do?"

Jeremy stated with confidence, "I fucked her best friend now we're even and we have the best marriage ever."

Harold let out a small laugh. "Great I am glad it worked out for you."

"I like you Harold, stay. You're the only honest, polite guy I have ever known."

"Not for long that will all change," Harold said as he left the office.

Harold worked the rest of the week managing to ignore Mark. Finally his last day came and he was more than happy to pack up his desk. As he was heading out the door, he ran into Mark.

"Excuse me," Harold said, maneuvering around Mark.

"Come on man! You can't leave this way we have had worst fights than this."

"Mark all my life I have been a big joke to every one I know. You only hang around because you can get a laugh off here and there at my expense."

Mark shook his head. "You make my day Harold. I feel lost without you man. This week has been torture. And then not seeing you anymore… come on you have been like a brother to me."

"You've been right calling me stupid all these years and it's time for me to get myself together."

"I don't mean it that way."

"Mark I've always envied you. You have always been the lady's man, and I always wanted to be like you."

"Wow man, thank you."

"Now I'm starting a new life. No more Harold its Harry now. Big tough strong Harry." Harold stood proud straightening his back. Suddenly the bottom of his box broke due to the water of the fish tank spilling and making it weak.

"Oh great!" Harold yelled.

Mark tried to help him but Harold just shooed him away. "Just go back to your desk, I'm fine."

He said it, but deep down he wasn't sure if he believed it.

Chapter Four

HAROLD DECIDED SINCE he was making a clean start he also needed to change his apartment as well. The new apartment was set up the same as his old one; the only difference was the walls were painted green. Harold felt a sense of accomplishment when he finished organizing his furniture.

"Yeah, things are going to be different now," he whispered sucking his teeth.

One morning as he walked outside he ran into an old friend, an oriental man whom owned a small deli where Harold bought coffee.

"Good Morning Mr. Hun," Harold greeted.

"Aaaah, Good Morning Harold," Mr. Hun said through his thick Asian accent.

"I was on my way by your place to get some coffee."

"No," he insisted. "No more coffee. Me selling it."

His accent was so heavy it was almost hard for Harold to catch what he meant.

"Why are you selling Mr. Hun?"

"I go back to my country, get married."

Harold shook Mr. Hun's hand. "Congratulations I'm happy to hear that."

"I can not find anyone to buy."

"Well if I hear of some one who is interested I'll let you know."

"Here my number." Mr. Hun wrote his number on a piece of paper and handed it to Harold. As Harold walked away, he thought to himself it would be a great idea to own the place. He ran after Mr. Hun grabbed him and told him his idea of buying the business himself. The next day Harold met up with Mr. Hun at his store. He anxiously showed him around the place. Harold was excited he really wanted to take the chance. He made the deal with the owner and a month later the store was his.

Harold had been saving money to buy a house during his marriage, which he gladly poured into building his bagel shop he proudly named: Harry's Bagel's. As days passed business quickly picked up and Harold found himself busier than he could've imagined. This was just the change he had needed; it kept his mind off of Linda. Having employees respect him made him feel he finally had authority.

Months went by and Harold seemed to be on the right track. He was quickly becoming successful in his business and gaining respect from people in the community. Despite his huge turnaround, he was still lonely and it was getting harder and harder to go home to an empty apartment every night.

One night as he was surfing the net he came across an ad for LOVE.COM. He hesitated for a moment before clicking on it, but figured what did he have to lose if he didn't. Since Harold did not enjoy the bar and club scenes he figured this was his only option. He clicked on the link for a new account and quickly filled out a profile listing all his information. After he finished he found his digital camera and took a few pictures of himself. One was in a suit; another was in jeans and a plain T-shirt. After reviewing his information he submitted it all and felt a twinge of anticipation. He went to bed hoping that soon enough he would have an email box full of responses.

A few days went by and Harold hadn't got any hits. He was starting to think that once again, he had made a fool of himself.

At the bagel shop he was up to his elbows in lattes and bagels with cream cheese. As he maneuvered behind the counter, counting out change and passing customers their cups he almost didn't notice Linda in the midst of the crowd.

"Harold, why haven't you signed the papers?" she hissed. The customers all turned around to stare at her.

"No, I haven't had a chance. I'm kind of busy."

"Well you need to get a move on it. I have to get married soon the baby is on its way!"

Linda was noticeably pregnant and Harold had learned she was now living with her lover. He hadn't signed the divorce papers yet, and he didn't have a clear reason why he hadn't. Seeing her the way she was, gave him all the confirmation he needed.

"Do you have them on you? I'll sign them now," he said as he passed a customer their change.

With pep in her step, Linda rushed out the door toward her car.

"That bitch! I can't believe her. She already has a new husband and a baby on the way," Harold explained to his employee Debra.

Debra was in her late fifties and she was a great employee. Harold relied on her completely ever since she had started working for him. Harold confided everything to her.

"She is moving on Harold, and it's time you do the same."

Debra said.

Harold looked past Debra to the mini-tornado that was Linda coming back in the door. She had papers in hand waving them like a crazy person.

"Here are the papers sign them please!"

She placed the papers in front of Harold and he stared down at them like they were written in Chinese. He hesitated to sign them; however, he knew Debra was right; it was time for him to move on. Signing the papers broke his heart considering now there was no reason to see her anymore. He quickly scribbled his name on the line she had so conveniently marked with an "X" and shoved them back across the counter to her.

"Thank you Harold," she said happily. "Take care."

He watched her bounce out of the shop as if she didn't have a care in the world taking his only care in the world with her.

After closing the bagel shop Harold walked Debra to her bus stop. Debra was also divorced however; she always found a way to see the brighter side of things and tried to keep Harold from making mistakes.

"Harry you look miserable cheer up," Debra said stopping in front of the bus stop.

"She was all I had to look forward too."

"Snap out of it!" Debra slapped Harold in the face lightly. "Are you crazy she's getting remarried and is having another man's baby and you're *still* thinking about her," Debra scolded.

"Ever since I was young I couldn't get a female to look at me, and then when I found Linda I was happy. I felt complete she was my soul mate. For a long time the best thing that ever happened to me."

Debra rolled her eyes. "No, she is *not* your soul mate. She is gone, over done with, move on! Why don't you go out and meet someone?"

"I do not know how? I wouldn't even know where to begin."

Debra's bus pulled up to the curb with a hiss. She turned to Harold. "Go get some rest and I will see you in the morning."

Back at his apartment Harold checked his answer machine and came up empty. He quickly remembered the profile he set up on LOVE.com and logged onto his computer. His mind was still on Linda and her swollen belly. The thought of her with another man made him want to hit something, but Debra was right, she had moved on and now he had to do likewise.

When he opened his mailbox, his heart jumped at the sight of the tiny envelope, signaling he had a message. He took a deep breath and double clicked his way to his new life.

He smiled as he read the message:

"Hi my name is Jenny write back to me I am very interested in meeting you, I love to have fun and I'm very outgoing meet me you will not be disappointed."

Her picture was very appealing. She had long straight black hair and a sun-kissed caramel complexion. He responded immediately and left his phone number hoping she would call.

Harold felt his mood slowly changing. As he began to clean up his apartment, he truly felt things could actually turn around for him. Just as he finished vacuuming, the phone rang. It was Jenny from LOVE.com.

"Hello Harold," she purred into the phone.

He felt his face flush hot with his own blush. "Hi Jenny. I'm glad you called."

"I can't believe you answered me so quickly," she giggled.

"I was surprised you were interested," he said.

"Do you have any plans tomorrow?" she asked.

"No not at all."

"Would you like to meet?" she asked confidently.

"Of course," he said, trying not to sound anxious.

"Wonderful."

"Where do you want to meet?"

"I love to eat seafood," she answered.

"Great so do I, actually I know a nice place."

"Perfect."

Chapter Five

THE NEXT DAY, Harold could barely concentrate at work. Debra noticed his ever-present smile and joked with him about it every chance she got. He didn't want to tell her about Jenny just yet, he wanted to feel Jenny out first, and make sure she wasn't nuts.

"Come on Harold, what's up? Where did this new attitude come from?" she asked.

"No reason," he smiled. "I'm just taking your advice."

She playfully pushed him in the back of his head. "Whatever Harold."

Harold prepared for his date as if it was his first. He was meticulous in picking out his outfit and took his time ironing and picking the right shoes.

He was admiring his choices in the mirror when the phone rang.

"Hello."

"Hey Harold, it's me Jenny."

"Do not tell me you lost your directions?"

"No," she hesitated. "I have to cancel our date I am sorry Harold."

He sank down on the couch, suddenly not caring if he wrinkled his pants or scuffed his shoes.

"Harold, you there?"

"I'm here," he said, trying not to let his disappointment show.

"We can try again next week since I'll be away on business this week."

"No problem," he replied.

"I promise I'll call you next week."

"I'll be here."

"Talk to you next week," she said before hanging up.

Harold sighed as he removed his clothes and slipped into his pajamas.

The next morning before leaving for work, Harold turned on his computer to check his emails. He was surprised to see he had an email from someone else. There was no picture but she claimed to be a 33-year-old dancer and her name was Sandy. Harold hesitated for a second, then went ahead and replied before running out the door. He figured it couldn't hurt.

"How was your date last night?" Debra asked.

"Cancelled," he replied.

He noticed the pity in her eyes, but he turned away so their eyes did not lock.

"No way what happened?" she asked.

"Work I guess."

"You guess? You didn't ask?"

"No, after I heard she had to cancel I blocked out the rest of the conversation."

"Great," Debra said, rolling her eyes. "You are horrible at communicating. Why didn't you ask?"

"What was there to ask? She couldn't go out, end of story."

"Harold next time she calls, ask questions. The more you show interest the more you learn, and the more they will like you."

"Why am I such a sucker?" he whined, leaning against the counter.

"You're not a sucker. You need to be more out going. Talk more; make women interested, don't just sit there like a bump on a log."

"You're right, you're right."

Harold reached over and burned his finger in the toaster. He wasn't paying attention when he stuck the bagel in and his finger went inside. Debra grabbed him and bandaged him up, shaking her head at her clumsy boss.

Harold arranged to meet Sandy at a restaurant not far from his apartment. He was so nervous that he wouldn't even talk to her on the phone. He instead arranged everything online.

At the restaurant he felt a small pang of relief when he realized that she hadn't showed up yet. He figured he could use the time to calm his nerves. A few moments later a tall, busty, big-shouldered woman approached his table. She had long curly red hair and sharp facial large features. Her makeup was over the top, accentuating every thing about her face that Harold didn't like. There was a lot to be said about pictures on the Internet and accuracy wasn't one of them. But then again he remembered she didn't have a picture in her profile, just a description.

He silently made a note to himself, "I'll have to ask for a picture for now on that's for sure."

"Hi Harold I am Sandy you look exactly like your picture," she said as she sat down.

"Nice to meet you," Harold said, wishing he could say the same.

Her hair was red and she had long huge eyelashes. There was something strange about the woman Harold thought. Even her voice seemed odd.

The waiter walked over to take their order and even he stared at the woman in horror. "Can I take your order?" the young man asked, never taking his eyes off her.

Harold replied quickly, "Ladies first."

"Let me see," she purred. "Ooh this sausage sounds good, let me have the sausage," She said licking her lips.

A wave of nausea washed over Harold. He wanted to jump up and bolt away from the table and out the restaurant but he was frightened. As he looked at her face, neck and arms, he could not help but to notice they had a manly, muscular tone to them.

The waiter turned to Harold. "What will you have?"

Harold hesitated. "I'll have the hamburger deluxe."

The waiter scurried toward the kitchen. Harold wanted to beg him to stay with him for support, but felt like that was over the top.

"Well tell me about your self," Sandy finally said.

"I own my own business," Harold started. "I work a lot." He looked her over again. "A whole lot."

"OOH so do I," she said proudly. "I work constantly. I dance and move my body left and right up, and down."

Sandy started gyrating and wiggling in her chair and everyone started looking.

"I get the picture," Harold said trying to get her to stop. He was hoping that the waiter would come out with the food so he could end his date, but he had no such luck.

Sandy blurted out. "Harold are you a freak?"

Harold choked and spit out the water he was drinking. "What do you mean by freak?" Harold whispered.

The waiter showed up and started placing their food in front of them.

"You know crazy sex, like a man," she said.

The waiter heard her and stopped arranging the food and quickly disappeared back through the swinging kitchen doors. Harold noticed him peeking through the window on the door.

"A man?" Harold's voice went up two octaves higher than he liked.

"Give me your hand Harold" Sandy demanded, gripping Harold's hand tightly. It was hard for Harold to let go as Sandy forced his hand on his lap. Harold jumped up, knocking down the table and ran out of the restaurant.

Back at his apartment, Harold tried to shake off what had just happened. If that was in the dating pool, he may have just taken his last dip. He noticed a message on his answer machine and listened reluctantly.

"Hello Harold it is me Jenny I am calling from the hotel I am staying in. I was bored I needed someone to talk to. I guess you are not home I will call you sometime tomorrow."

Harold quickly erased the message. After his terrible date he wasn't in the mood to deal with another nutcase.

He went into his closet and tossed his shoes in and found his box full of pictures of Linda and him. He flipped thru them smiling and thinking of the good old times. All too quickly he remembered what she had done and anger took over as he threw the pictures in the sink and burned them to a crisp. He went into his bedroom turned out the lights and fell asleep.

The next morning he was walking out of the house to go to work. The phone rang stopping his rush to the bagel shop.

"Hello Harold, it's me Jenny."

Something about her voice made Harold melt, his mind blocked all other thoughts when he spoke to her.

"Hey Jenny," he said, smiling. "How are you?"

"Good I am still here finishing up with work. It has been so hectic."

"Yeah I know the feeling."

"I work with monsters all day," Jenny laughed.

Harold laughed. "Oh yeah that is how I feel too sometimes."

"Well I have to go open the shop," Harold said.

"Can I call you tonight?" Jenny asked softly.

"I would like that," Harold said.

"Okay, then I will talk to you later."

Chapter Six

HAROLD RAN STRAIGHT home after work. He definitely didn't want to miss Jenny's call, so he let Debra close up and headed home.

For five hours he waited.

It was almost 10:00 pm and she still hadn't called. He sat on the couch and started to get upset. He was falling into the same trap he had with Linda. He got up and turned on his computer to check if anyone else responded to his personal ad. He made up his mind that from now on he was going to take a page out of Mark's book.

He was surprised to see that another woman had answered him online. Against his better judgment he arranged to meet her. At this point he didn't care what happened or who showed up.

He powered down his computer around 1:00 am and still had no call from Jenny. Feeling rejected he decided to go to bed.

He met his next date at a movie theater. He let her make the plans this time; he didn't care where they ended up. He stood outside the movie theatre secretly hoping that she didn't show. Just then a beat up minivan pulled up and the driver waved to him. She pulled the van into a parking space and hopped out, almost running towards Harold.

"Hi my name is Anne," she said full of energy.

She was a bubbly blonde.

"Nice to meet you Anne," he said, forcing a smile.

"I'll be right back," she said heading back towards her van.

He watched as she opened the rear door and five children piled out yelling and fighting. She hoisted a two year old up to her shoulder screaming and the other four trailed behind her. They were three boys and two girls. They repeatedly pulled each other's hair and took swings at one another.

"Listen I am sorry my baby-sitter couldn't make it and I didn't want to cancel the date," she started to explain. "I have not been out in a while, so I hope you don't mind."

Harold eyeballed the screaming children. He didn't want to be rude and run off so he tried to make the best of it.

"What do you want to see?" he yelled over the screeches and wails of the kids.

The kids screamed that they wanted to watch a cartoon, which was the last thing Harold wanted to see. Unfortunately nothing their mother said would change their minds. Reluctantly, Harold followed them into the movie theater chasing after the young one who made a beeline for a different theatre.

After he got them seated, he ended up spending over $100 dollars on candy, popcorn and sodas. Through out the movie, they spilled soda on him, yelled constantly, spit on him and wouldn't sit still. Finally, the two-year-old girl peed on him.

He jumped up. "I am sorry Anne, I gotta go."

He left her and her unruly kids in the movie theatre.

When he got home he filled the tub and sank into the hot water letting it soothe his tense muscles. He thought back to the scene at the movie theatre and couldn't help but laugh to himself.

A few moments later the phone rang. He jumped out of the tub and slid on the floor landing on his butt before making it to the phone.

"Hello."

"Hey Harold, it's me, Jenny."

Taking the cordless receiver with him he slid back into the warmth of the water and let her voice soothe him. "Hey, how's it going?"

"I am at the airport, getting ready to go home. I can't wait. I am so tired."

"Good, you'll be able to relax," he said trying hard to keep her on the phone. Just talking to her made him feel better. It was just what he needed to forget his horrid date.

"Yeah, I know. I have had a crazy week," she said. "Hey I want to apologize for not calling you. Do you think we can get together tomorrow at my place? I'll even cook."

His mind hit rewind as he relived his last two experiences. He definitely wasn't in the mood for another crazy evening. "I'm not sure Jenny, It's been crazy at the bagel shop and I'm really tired."

"I really want to meet you, please," she begged.

He took a deep breath, and figured he had nothing to lose. "What time?"

At work the next day Debra laughed hysterically as Harold told her about Anne and her children.

"I can't believe you got pissed on," she laughed.

"Well tonight I'm meeting the last one then I'm removing myself from the Internet," He said.

"I can't wait to see how this turns out," Debra said, still laughing.

"Shut up." Harold laughed, flicking water in her face playfully.

The rest of the day Harold was too busy to obsess over his impending date. No matter how much Debra picked at him about it during the day, he tried hard to ignore her remarks about all the things that could go wrong as he busied himself with customers.

At 8p.m. he drove straight to Jenny's house. He rang the bell and immediately felt like he had made a mistake. Harold had rehearsed several excuses to leave, just incase she turned out to be just as crazy as his first date. Just when he was about to leave, the door flew open and he was face to face with a giant green lizard.

Harold jumped and screamed, causing him to fall down her front steps. Jenny removed her lizard mask and hurried to help him up.

"Oh my goodness," she laughed. "I'm so sorry! Are you okay?"

"Yeah, I'm fine," he said, trying to pretend he hadn't hurt his knee.

He looked into her face and forgot all his pain.

She was beautiful. Her skin was flawless and her eyes were hypnotizing. Her smile was enough to make him forget that he had just tumbled down her front steps. She took him by the hand and led him into the house.

Once inside he noticed there were costumes and monster masks everywhere.

"I didn't realize you already had company," he joked, picking up one of the masks.

"I make costumes for a movie company," she said.

"Oh, okay."

"I guess I forgot to mention that to you last week. We filmed a horror movie so I had to go dress my monster." She laughed.

"This is awesome! I loved these things when I was younger," he said holding up a gruesome mask.

Jenny smiled. "Let me get the dinner have a seat."

While she was in the kitchen, he took a chance to look around. Other than the costumes and masks, she had a really nice home. Nothing that would've suggested she had just escaped a mental hospital. He was looking through a photo album that had pictures of her with actors and movie props when she appeared in the dining room with a pan of lasagna.

"That smells awesome."

"Thanks. I hope you like it. I love to cook but I don't have anyone to cook for," she said, placing a huge piece on his plate.

"You can cook for me anytime," he said.

She took a seat across the table from him and they shared small talk over salad and some of the most delicious lasagna Harold had ever tasted. He tried hard not to inhale his food in front of her, but she was a great cook.

"I'm glad we finally got to meet," she said. "I was a little leery about meeting over the internet."

"Trust me, I understand." Harold started to tell her about his other dates, but decided against it.

"You think I have monsters in here, you'd be surprised by some of the creatures I've met on the Internet," she said laughing.

Harold felt himself becoming more and more relaxed with her. They both had so much in common.

Jenny lived with someone for ten years before he left her. And like him, she was looking for an honest caring relationship.

After dinner they moved to the living room, where they drank wine, laughed and talked some more. They shared their horror stories from the Internet and Harold told her the story behind his broken marriage.

"Wow, I'm so sorry," Jenny, said, placing her hand on his.

"It's okay; things are definitely looking up for me."

Harold leaned in and kissed Jenny softly on the lips before suddenly jerking away.

"I'm sorry," he mumbled, setting his glass on the table. "I guess I need to go."

She smiled and walked him to the door.

"Thank you for coming Harold I had a really nice time."

"I did too."

This time she leaned in to kiss him and he didn't jerk away.

Chapter Seven

"So, HOW'D IT go lover boy?"

Harold shot Debra a look, but he was way too happy to let her get to him.

He smiled. "I think I met the most perfect woman in the world."

"No kids?"

"Nope."

"No crazy sex habits?"

He winked. "Not that I know of."

Debra laughed. "Well I'm happy for you."

Over the next couple of days Harold and Jenny spoke every night and went out every weekend. He would surprise her on the set from time to time and they would go out to lunch. She started coming by the bagel shop regularly and Debra gave her stamp of approval. She was delighted that Harold was finally happy.

The moments he made love to Jenny made him feel strong and proud. Harold felt as if he found his true soul mate. Christmas felt like a holiday again.

A year went by fast and Harold finally felt complete.

One day while they were out eating he heard a voice calling from the other side of the room. He turned around and it was Mark. He hadn't seen him in almost two years.

"Hey man, what's up? Long time no see."

"How you been?"

Mark bear hugged Harold. "I missed you."

"I tried calling you a few times but your cell is disconnected," Harold said.

"This is Nina and she knows all about how such a great friend you have always been to me," Mark said introducing his date.

"This is Jenny," Harold proudly gestured.

"Nice to meet you." Mark said, shaking her hand.

"Nina and I are engaged," Mark announced.

"Aw man, Congratulations!"

Nina showed every one her ring. Harold and Jenny smiled. Jenny moved closer to Nina. She held up her hand, showing off her ring.

"That's very pretty," Jenny cooed, examining it closer.

"Harold can I talk to you," Mark asked.

"What's up?"

Mark eyed Jenny and Nina, chatting about wedding stuff. He turned to Harold. "Take a walk with me outside."

"Excuse us ladies," Harold said.

Harold followed Mark past the waiter stand and out to the front doors of the restaurant. They were immediately over-taken with smokers who had been abolished from the restaurant.

"Harold I just wanted to apologize about what went down between us," Mark explained.

"Mark it's cool. I don't care about the past. I'm a new person and I'm in love. I also own a business. So I'm good."

"Wow man, you own a business?"

"Yeah, I bought a deli and turned it into a bagel shop. It's not that far from my apartment."

"That's good man. I'm happy for you." Mark patted Harold on the back.

"Thanks man."

"Harold it's so good to see you again," Mark, said hugging him

"Yeah, I'm glad I ran into you."

The next morning, Harold was preparing the shop to open when Linda walked in. She had cut her hair and dyed it dark brown. He could tell she had lost a little weight.

"Hello Harold."

Harold smiled at the toddler clinging to her body.

"Hey Linda what are you doing here?"

"I was in the neighborhood and I decided to stop in."

Debra was pretending to sweep the floor, but Harold knew she was listening to their conversation.

"What can I get you?" Harold asked wiping down the counter.

Linda followed him around. "Harold I made a mistake leaving you."

Harold nervously dropped a crate full of cream cheese. "You come back saying you made a mistake!" Harold spat. "What is wrong with you?"

"Harold I have been feeling guilty since the first day I left you."

The desperation in her voice was annoying Harold more than anything.

"What do you want from me? You left me remember. You were tired and needed a change and that's what you got."

"I want you back Harry I miss you."

"What about your husband? Doesn't your son need his father?"

"You'll be a better father to him. Please Harold, I made a mistake. I need you."

Harold tosses the cloth he was using onto the counter. "It's too late Linda. I don't feel anything for you, and I have someone else who I am very much in love with. She loves me for the person I am and because of her I've become a better person."

"You still love me. Come on remember old times?" Linda puckered up her lips trying to seduce Harold.

Harold stared at Linda with a look of disbelief.

"It's over Linda. Hell, it's been over. You need to go home to your husband."

She sucked her teeth. "Your loss Harold. Your new love will never care about you the way I do."

"Linda you never cared about me, I was just a convenience to you."

"You're wrong Harold."

Debra cleared her throat as customers began walking into the shop.

"I don't have time for this Linda."

Harold watched her storm out and he breathed a sigh of relief as he watched her climb into her car and drive away.

"I'm so proud of you," Debra said hugging him.

"I can't believe her!" Harold clapped his hands together.

"The nerve of that woman Harold. You know what she is up to? Her new man left and now she needs some one to support her and that kid."

"You're probably right Deb, but my heart belongs to Jenny."

Harold left the shop early and headed to Jenny's. He stopped along the way and bought the biggest, prettiest bouquet of flowers he could find.

He smiled as he rang her doorbell. The fact that Linda had tried to come crawling back boosted his self-esteem a few notches.

"Oh wow what is the occasion?" Jenny asked when she opened the door.

"Do I have to have a reason to buy you flowers?"

She hugged him and tried to avoid getting the green slime she had all over her hands on him.

"Slimy and all you still make my heart beat." They kissed lovingly. "You're the prettiest woman I ever seen."

"I guess I can let you in then."

As she put the flowers in water he told her about his day.

"I saw my crazy ex-wife today and I realized just how lucky I am to have met you."

"That's so sweet, thank you. I feel the same way about you."

The rest of the afternoon Harold stayed and helped Jenny put her creature together since she had a deadline. He stood in place as she tried the costume on him. They both had a perfect understanding and their relationship meant so much to both of them. Harold felt like he may have gotten it right this time.

Chapter Eight

AT SIX O'CLOCK THE next morning Harold's cell phone rang. He smiled when he woke up beside Jenny.

He checked the Caller ID and it was Mark.

"Get up boy!" Mark laughed.

"I'm awake now that you are yelling in my ear," he said. "What's up?"

"Let's go fishing like the old days," Mark said.

"Now?" Harold asked, trying not to wake Jenny.

"Yes now, come on."

"Okay. Gimmie a few minutes."

"I'll be outside in five minutes, don't fall back to sleep."

"I'll be ready."

Jenny woke up and stretched against Harold's body.

"I like waking up with you," she said

Harold kissed her. "Likewise."

A few minutes later they heard Mark's horn blaring outside.

"Who is that?" Jenny asked.

Harold walked over to the window. "I can't believe he is here already. That guy is nuts!"

Where are you going?" Jenny asked as Harold pulled on some jeans and a top.

"Mark asked me to go fishing," he yelled to her as he jolted to the bathroom to wash his face, and brush his teeth. "I'll call you when we get back."

Out the door he went.

"Smell the air it's refreshing," Mark said when they arrived at the dock.

Mark had on a big fishing hat with fishing hooks and emblems hanging from it.

"What are you wearing that for?" Harold laughed.

"This is my good luck charm."

They found a comfortable spot and set up. Harold couldn't put the fishing line together and ended up getting all tangled up. Mark finally helped him put it together correctly. As Harold extended the rod to throw it into the water, he latched the fishing hook onto Marks hat. It was stuck and as he tried to free it on the hook Harold accidentally threw it across into the water. Mark stared in shock as his hat hit the water.

"Just great," Mark said.

Harold laughed. "My bad."

When they finally got situated Mark turned to Harold.

"Harold I want to ask you something important."

"What is it?" Harold asked.

"We finally set the wedding date. It's going to be in two months."

"Wow that is fantastic. I never thought you had it in you."

"Well I had never found the right one."

"I am so happy for both of you," Harold said, hugging Mark.

"Well, I want you to be my best man," Mark asked as he reached in the cooler taking out two beer bottles.

Harold tried to mask his shock. "You want me to be your best man." Mark rose to hand Harold a beer as the two men cheered causing Harold to fall over the ledge and into the water.

Chapter Nine

JENNY ARRIVED LATE from work. She started searching for her keys because she did not hear them jingling in her pocketbook.

"Excuse me." A woman tapped Jenny on the back.

When Jenny turned around Linda stood there looking pathetic with the baby sleeping in her arms.

"Oh my goodness are you okay?" Jenny asked.

"I need to speak to you," Linda whispered.

"Me?" Jenny asked. "Do I know you?"

"You don't know me, but it's about my husband, Harold," Linda said.

"Your *husband*?"

"Look, can I come in?" Linda asked.

Jenny's heart was pounding as she opened the door. She couldn't believe this was happening.

Linda followed her inside and laid her son down on the couch.

"Okay, what's going on?" Jenny demanded.

"I am so sorry to have to spring this on you like this."

Jenny sat down cautiously.

Linda eyeballed her then asked, "What's your name?"

"Jenny."

"Jenny I am sorry to bother you in your home but I do feel you have a right to know."

"A right to know what?" Jenny asked, her agitation rising.

"Harold is married. We've been married for eight years. Some time last year he walked out on me and our son Jonathan."

Tears stung Jenny's eyes. "What are you talking about?"

"I have been following him around and I found you."

Jenny couldn't say a word as she fought hard to keep the tears from rolling down her cheeks.

"I am sorry, but I needed closure in order for me to go on. He is horrible. He left us deserted and penniless," Linda continued with her lie. "I have no home because of him. I just wanted to warn you, he is a pig," Linda said.

Linda stood to her feet and prepared to leave. Jenny wasn't sure she could stand, but she managed to get up enough strength to walk her to the door.

Linda stopped and said, "Please, be careful so you don't end up like me."

Without a word Jenny closed the door behind her and suddenly wished she had never met Harold.

The next day Harold tried relentlessly to get in touch with Jenny, but she wasn't returning his calls. He began to worry so he ran to her apartment to see what was wrong. When he arrived he came up empty there as well.

He tried calling again on his way back to the bagel shop but got her voicemail. He new something was strange since they normally would speak several times a day.

As Harold served customers, he kept checking his cell hoping to hear from Jenny. He didn't want to appear concerned, but he must have because Debra finally asked him what was wrong.

"Why do you keep checking that phone?" Debra asked

"I haven't heard from Jenny all day and that's not like her."

"She's probably busy with work, have you called her?"

"I have, but I keep getting voicemail."

"The problem is she got you by the balls."

"That's not true. Especially since the last woman to get me like that left me."

"Well then don't worry she'll call when she gets a chance."

"You're right."

Harold tried to busy himself the rest of the day and not think about Jenny. It was hard and he screwed up quite a few orders, but luckily his customers weren't angry with him.

"Can I have some coffee?"

Harold stopped in his tracks at the irritating voice.

"Linda, what are you doing here?"

"I would like a coffee and sweet, sweet just like Harry," she said flirting.

"I'll get it," Debra said.

"Thank you Deb I will be right back." Harold removed his plastic gloves and started towards the door.

"Where are you going I came here to see you?" Linda said grabbing Harold's hand.

Harold just laughed in her face and walked out of the shop.

Linda's eyes narrowed in frustration.

"What are you up to?" Debra asked.

"Excuse me?" Linda replied.

"Why are you here aggravating Harold?"

"Listen," Linda snapped. "You need to mind your own business."

"Harold *is* my business."

"HA, HA, HA, you better watch out because this place will be mine soon. I'm going to get my Harry back."

"It's too late for that."

"I think it is better that you stay out of this."

Linda grabbed her cup of coffee and walked out without paying.

Chapter Ten

HAROLD DROVE TO the movie set where Jenny was working. He parked his car and started wandering around the fake city, trying to find Jenny.

"Excuse me sir you can't come this way." A security officer told him.

"I am looking for someone," Harold said.

"That's all well and good, but you can't come in this area without proper identification."

"I will only be one minute I promise."

"I am sorry sir, you have to leave."

The guard grabbed Harold by his arm, that's when he noticed Jenny walking by with a crowd of people.

"That's her," he insisted. "Jenny!"

When she saw him she quickly turned the other way. Harold broke the guards grasp and ran after her.

"Jenny why are you avoiding me?"

She started helping an actor with his costume and tried to avoid him. "Just stay away from me."

"Why? What did I do?"

"You lied to me."

"Ready on the set!" A director yelled out.

"What did I lie about?" Harold asked.

Jenny looked in the direction of the voice. "I'm busy leave me alone and please do not bother me again."

"What is going on Jenny?"

Without answering Jenny just walked away. The security guard happily escorted Harold off the grounds.

As Harold walked out he noticed a monster costume hanging. He grabbed it off the rack and ducked into the bathroom.

He had a hard time putting it on but he finally tugged and shoved himself into the tight material. Harold wobbled his way out of the bathroom with the heavy lizard head weighing him down. He scanned the area for the security guard then headed back in the direction he had last seen Jenny.

"There you are! You're in this scene come on."

A man grabbed Harold's arm and lead him into a room that was made up to look like a swamp. A few moments later, two actors came in and started reading their lines. Harold slowly started to make a break for it when the director yelled at him.

"Hey!! Monster! Back to your spot!"

"Is the stunt man drunk again?" A crew member asked.

Harold stood patiently behind the trees as they directed him to do. He was supposed to come out and attack the actors. Instead he was excited to see Jenny, and ran to her knocking half the set down.

"Cut, cut this is horrible. Who hired the actor for the monster scene?" the director yelled.

"Help me," Harold yelled, trying to take his mask off.

Jenny helped him pull off the mask.

"What are you doing?" she asked furiously.

"I need to talk to you."

"I believe that is mine." An under-dressed actor approached Harold and snatched the lizard head.

"Oh yeah, I am so sorry."

Harold wrestled his way out of the hot material.

Jenny tried to help him as Harold fell to the floor. When the suit was finally off security escorted him out of the filming area. Jenny continued to work as if he had never been there.

Harold drove back to the bagel shop and Debra was still there cleaning.

"What happened?" Debra asked when she saw his face.

"I don't understand," Harold said, plopping down in a chair. "She called me a liar and doesn't want to see me anymore."

"Does this have anything to do with Linda?" Debra asked.

"What?"

"Linda," she repeated. "Today she came in here and told me this shop is going to be hers."

"What?"

"She claims her intentions are to get you back."

"I can't believe that bitch!"

Debra pushed him towards the door. "You have to go talk to her."

He immediately ran to Jenny's apartment and camped out on her front steps until she got home.

"What the heck are you doing here?" she snapped.

"Jenny please."

"Just leave!" she screamed.

"Wait can we talk about this?" he asked following her inside. "Jenny please what did I do wrong?"

Jenny threw her keys on the table and tossed her jacket on the couch, still not acknowledging him.

"Talk to me I need to know what is wrong?" Harold pleaded.

Jenny faced him with tears in her eyes. "Harold I don't have the strength to explain myself."

"I don't understand," Harold said. "We were doing so good."

Jenny sank down on a chair. "I have been hurt too many times and I can't deal with this. Please just go back to your wife leave me alone."

Jenny stood up and walked to the front door. "Get out now!" she yelled furiously.

"Jenny I'm divorced! I don't have a wife."

"Just go Harold. I know about men like you, cheaters, liars, you thought you could get away with it. I do not think so." Jenny grabbed Harold by the arm and pushed him out the door.

"Jenny what has gotten into you?"

Jenny slammed the door in Harold's face and turned up the volume to her stereo to drown out him banging on the door. He gave up and walked to a near by park.

It was very dark outside and he was a little nervous because the neighborhood was full of unruly teens. As he stopped for the red light to cross the street he noticed his jeep drive by him with two males driving he had never seen before. As he ran after it screaming he tripped over his shoelaces and the thieves got away laughing at him.

Harold miserably looked at a couple kissing on a bench before walking over to a swing sitting down. He looked up at the moon and shook his head.

"I am so pathetic!" he yelled.

"Shut up man!" A voice yelled back at him. Harold looked to see a couple making love upon a park bench about 50 yards in back of him.

Suddenly the police arrived at the park to chase every one out. The police officers told the couple to leave the park since it was late and the park closed at a certain time.

Harold walked over to the police officer. "Excuse me officer," Harold said frantically.

"Yeah what is it," he asked chewing gum.

"My jeep was just stolen and I have no way to get home," Harold explained.

"When did this happen?" the officer asked.

"About twenty minutes ago. I was parked two blocks away and I decided to take a walk to clear my mind. A few moments later I noticed two young guys driving away with my car." Harold said.

"Okay let me take a report."

"Can you guys give me a ride home?"

"Alright come on get in the car explain the story as we drive."

Harold slid into the back seat of the police cruiser. His nostrils stung from the stench rising from the worn leather seats. He imagined all the criminals that had been in that backseat before him.

The overweight cop that was driving slid into the front seat causing it to scream under his weight. "Okay, Mr. Lucky, where do you live?"

The next day Harold felt worse than he did when Linda left him. He woke up washed his face and reluctantly made his way to the bagel shop. Customers were lined up out the door as they waited patiently for Debra to fix their orders.

"Harold what happened you're late?"

"I'm sorry Debra, I had a rough night and I over slept. It's over between Jenny and I," Harold said pouring himself a cup of coffee.

"Wow, are you sure?" Debra asked. "She is just mad, give her some time she may come around."

"I don't know where she got the idea that I have a wife," Harold said as he sipped his coffee burning his mouth.

"Listen I am old and wise and let me tell you, your ex is behind this," Debra said.

"Where would Jenny see Linda?" Harold asked.

"Hey you never know with Linda."

"I don't think so. Jenny has to be jumping to conclusions."

"Take my advice Linda is up to something."

"I'm going to go by Jenny's house, maybe she's in a better mood today."

"Who is going to help me in here?" Debra shrieked.

"You're a big girl you can handle it," Harold yelled as he ran out of the bagel shop.

Chapter Eleven

AS JENNY WAITED in the airport for her flight she sobbed as she slid her shades on.

"Hey Jenny, I didn't recognize you with those glasses on," Stefan said as he walked toward her.

Stefan was a tall man in his fifties with salt and pepper hair and a heavy moustache.

"Oh hello Mr. Reilly," Jenny said removing her glasses.

"Is every thing alright?"

"I'm fine just tired."

"We have a lot of work to do we're shooting this movie in Egypt a month away from home is that why you are sad?"

"No I am prepared for that actually my creation is perfect I shipped him to the studio already it is going to be awesome. It's just allergies I am ready to go," Jenny said reassuring herself.

"Well we'll be working together on this so I know it is going to be stunning." Stefan grinned.

"Airline 226 direct flight to Egypt now boarding gate 13."

The woman's voice boomed over the loud speaker, causing Jenny to flinch.

"That's us," Stefan said walking over to the gate.

"Let's go," Jenny said taking a deep breath. Her heart ached so bad she thought she was going to pass out. She missed Harold but she knew he belonged to someone else and had to get him out of her mind. Jenny grabbed her bag and walked onto the airplane and discreetly wiped the tears from her eyes.

When Harold arrived at Jenny's apartment, he rang her bell relentlessly, but didn't get an answer. A woman was coming down the steps and he stopped her.

"Excuse me ma'am, do you know Jenny Reston? She lives in this building," he asked.

"Yes I do what you want from her?" she asked suspiciously.

"It is important that I speak to her."

"Well, she's not here. I saw her leave this morning and she had luggage."

"Where did she go?"

"I do not know she just asked me to pick up her mail."

"Okay, thank you."

After a few days went by Harold found himself back at square one: lonely and depressed. He even started avoiding the bagel shop. He stopped shaving and his apartment was a mess. Beer bottles and empty takeout containers were all over the floor.

Harold had just settled in on his couch with a beer and a bag of chips when there was a knock at his door. He contemplated not answering but did anyway.

He tried to act happy to see his friend Mark when he opened the door.

"Hey man what is going on? I just went to the bagel shop. Debra told me every thing," Mark said as he hugged Harold.

Harold reclaimed his place on the couch. "I came to a conclusion since I have been locked in here for three days, no more crying that's it. I loved Jenny more than Linda and she didn't love me back. I'm going on a woman hunt, not a woman to fall in love with. I want women just to occupy my time and lust. Mark I'm going to have a different one every night, the way I change my underwear I'm going to change women."

Harold got up and walked over to his desk opening the drawer. He pulled out paper and searched for a pen knocking over plants and books.

"Take it easy!" Mark laughed. "You're not going to find a woman in there."

"I am making a chart counting all the women I sleep with," Harold explained.

"Well I'm glad to see you are handling this breakup better," Mark said.

"I'm in my thirties and I have only been with three women, that's crazy! Why should I be loyal and honest?

Fuck that!" Harold rambled, scribbling some notes on the paper.

"Okay go take a shower and get dressed. I'm going to call Nina we are going out tonight. I haven't been out in a long time," Mark said.

"I don't want to get you in trouble," Harold laughed.

"Me? In trouble?" Mark boasted. "I make the decisions and rules in our relationship.

"Cool, then I'm going to take a shower and I'll be ready to go."

Mark and Harold arrived at Luxurious Ladies Nude bar.

Mark covered his face outside worried that some one would see him. Nina would flip if she knew he was there.

"I can't believe you dragged me to this place," Mark said. "I thought we were going to a club."

"Hey I didn't hear you argue with me when I suggested it," Harold said opening the door.

Harold walked in and immediately started hooting and hollering at the scantily clad women. Most of them looked at him like he was crazy and moved in the other direction.

"This is what I mean Mark that's right girls! Yeah!" Harold yelled like a maniac.

"Man, what has gotten into you?" Mark asked.

"OOOH you ain't seen nothing yet. I am going to put you to shame."

Harold was over the top. Mark stared at him bewildered at all the women in front of him slithering on the floor with oil all over their flesh. A woman sat on Harold's lap and began playing with his hair while he massaged her breasts.

"Harold you know you have to pay her right?" Mark asked.

He pulled out a handful of hundreds from his pocket and the woman got excited and started grinding even more on Harold. Mark got up from his seat and walked out, leaving Harold and his newfound friend.

Jenny was dressing an actor and she laughed to herself as she remembered Harold in the costume back on her other set. Jenny yearned for Harold he was the only man she felt happy with, he made her smile all the time. She dreaded the thought of starting all over again in the dating scene she had hoped Harold was the last man in her life.

She figured it wasn't meant to be and continued working on her actor's costume.

"Hello would you like a drink?" A tanned man with dark Arabian eyes asked.

"Thank you very much I would love it."

The man handed Jenny a bottle of water. "It is very hot here you know I have been watching you and you have not had anything to drink," he said with a heavy accent.

"I appreciate it, thanks for your concern," Jenny said politely

"My name is Mouhab." He extended his hand for her to shake.

"I'm Jenny," she said taking his hand.

"I know you are staying at my hotel The Sunrise," he said.

"Oh my goodness! That's your hotel? It's beautiful."

"Yes I accommodated your crew for the month. I have been watching the film and it's coming along great. It looks like it'll be a hit."

"I hope so I have been working hard on this one."

"I can't believe such a pretty and dainty woman can have such a frightening imagination."

"I love making these creations it's exciting."

"Would you like to join me later for a drink in the lounge?"

"Sure, why not? I'll see you later."

"Okay then, I guess I'll see you tonight."

Jenny wanted to get Harold out of her mind and planned on doing it in Egypt.

****

Harold wrote a big number one on his women chart proudly. His night with the stripper went fabulous and it was the best craziest sex he had ever had. The next morning he walked to the bagel shop prancing down the street like a gigolo proudly, although inside he craved to hear Jenny's voice.

"Good morning everyone," he said, smiling big.

He noticed Linda talking to Debra and his whole mood changed.

"What are you doing here?" he asked.

"I came to tell you how much I missed you," Linda winked.

Debra made vomiting gestures behind Linda's back.

"Linda you are such a slut, and...I love it!" Harold said grabbing her hands.

Debra stared at him in disbelief.

"Really Harry? Wow you're getting me excited," Linda flirted.

"Actually you are getting me excited Linda."

Debra went into the back area of the bagel shop leaving them alone.

"Harold why don't you come over to my place? I missed you over this past year. I miss the way you tickled me."

"What about your husband?"

"He won't be home until later."

"This is great; you can be number two on my list."

"What are you talking about?"

He chuckled. "Nothing lets go." Harold put his arm around Linda they headed out the door.

Ten minutes later they were at Linda's house.

"I have missed you so much Harry. Did you miss me?"

"No not really," he said. "I just want to have sex."

Linda cocked her head to the side. "What? You don't want me back."

"Let's not talk. Take off your clothes," he said, grabbing at her shirt. "There's no reason to talk "

"But I want to talk," she persisted. "How are you doing with that bagel shop? It seems to be doing really well."

Harold continued to ignore her and began lifting up her shirt and unhooking her bra.

"Harold you're an animal. You never did this when we were married."

He ignored her and continued kissing and touching her, slamming her down upon the bed and ravaging her like a mad man.

"Harold I never knew you had it in you," Linda said giving into his touch.

Harold pulled down his pants and was ready to make her his number two when Linda jumped up from the bed.

"Oh my goodness Harold Carl is here!"

"What? Who?" Harold asked, pulling his pants back up.

The bedroom door swung open and a tall large-framed man with blond hair and bushy eyebrows opened the door. His eyes turned red like a bull ready to charge causing Harold to turn white as a ghost.

"You little prick I'm gonna kill you!"

Carl lunged at Harold and he jumped over the bed. His pants were still wrapped around his knees. In one motion quickly he snatched them up running out the door.

Carl chased after him ripping off his hunting rifle which hung on a wall in the hallway. Linda tried to grab onto his big arm to stop him from hurting Harold but he tossed her like a rag doll. Harold sprinted around the house like a rabbit running for his life before he tripped down the whole flight of stairs, running into the kitchen and knocking dishes over. With Carl a few steps behind Harold ran back up the bedroom stairs and ended up in the bedroom with no way to escape. Harold decided to jump out the window. He landed on the ground onto a bunch of leaves, but he quickly jumped up running all the way home.

****

Jenny wore a white strapless dress and threw a red shawl over her shoulders, she thought about Harold when he spilled wine on her dress. Her thoughts caused her to rush to meet Mouhab sooner.

She entered the lounge of the hotel, which was done in an Arabic design. The hallways had big vases, silk drapes and beautiful rugs. Jenny took a seat on a big comfortable yellow couch and a woman brought a drink to her. Mouhab entered the room wearing what had to be an expensive silver suit with a burgundy silk button down shirt. Every finger on his hands had a ring on it.

Jenny began to feel intimidated by the wealthy sheik.

"Comfortable my dear Jenny?" he said slithering close to her.

Jenny slid over just a bit trying to put a little distance between them.

"Thank you for inviting me," she said nervously realizing his intentions. Mouhab ran his warm hand up her thigh caressing her leg through her dress.

"What do you think of this country? Isn't it lovely the warmth in the air, even at night."

"Yes, the weather is beautiful."

Mouhab smiled at her and licked his lips. "Oh you are perfect."

He worked his hand up her inner thigh and worked his fingers beyond the thin material of her panties, finding her center.

Jenny jumped up from the couch. "Please do not touch me!"

"But why?" he asked confused. "I thought you would like it considering you are a lonely American woman."

"What do you mean a lonely American woman? What makes you think I'm lonely?"

He stood to his feet. "You agreed to meet me tonight, so I assumed you were looking for the same thing I was."

"Actually I was looking to have a normal conversation. But I see that's not going to happen, especially with you."

"Please don't be offended with me I only wanted to be friendly."

"I'm going back to my room," Jenny said annoyed at the fact she had to face being a single woman again.

Jenny went to her room picked up the phone to call Harold and hung it up again crying herself to sleep.

The next few days Harold suffered from loneliness and the bar scenes were not working. He decided to sign onto Love.com again in hope to find a companionship not love. He just wanted someone to pass time. Harold cared for Jenny profoundly and did not want any one to take her place.

That evening he received a phone call from the police department saying that they located his jeep. Harold quickly called a cab and made his way to the impound lot. When he got there it was in very bad condition. The seats and tires were missing and it was painted graffiti in hot pink. He cringed at the sight of the condition of the vehicle he had driven for over ten years.

He decided to take a bus into town because there was no way he was driving a pink anything. He ended up at a Mercedes dealership in the heart of downtown. He figured it was time for something better and more attractive since the bagel shop profits were increasing.

After two hours of patronizing the sales clerk and test-driving cars, he decided on a silver Mercedes CLK 350 coupe. He sat in his new vehicle put on his sunglasses fixed his hair in the rear view mirror and drove out of the dealership with pride. He drove straight to Mark's house and began honking his horn loudly. Mark appeared from his door with a dishtowel over his shoulder and Nina behind him.

"Harold you bought a new car?" Mark laughed.

"Well what do you think?" Harold yelled.

"This car is gorgeous," Nina said running her fingers over the hood.

"Wow man, I can't believe you got rid of the old jeep."

"Very nice congratulations," Nina said giving Harold a kiss on his cheek.

"Thanks, well I got places to go, people to see," Harold said as he placed his sunglasses over his eyes.

Mark patted him on the shoulder. "Call me later."

"Will do."

As Harold opened the car door his alarm went off. The sound was so loud he began to panic. For a few seconds he fumbled with the keychain trying to figure out how to turn it off.

"How do you turn this off?" Mark said as he noticed his neighbors coming out of their houses.

"I have no idea," Harold said as he feverishly pressed buttons in the vehicle.

Finally, after ten minutes, Mark found the cut off switch and the alarm stopped.

"I think I should study the manual," Harold said.

"Yeah definitely," Mark agreed. "Well congratulations man I wish I could hang out with you but tonight we are having friends over for dinner." Mark said shaking Harold's hand.

"Sounds nice have a good time."

"Why don't you come by?" Mark asked.

"Nah, I really got to go," Harold lied as he jumped in his new car. "I'll call you later."

Harold drove around the city showing off his new shiny toy, but after an hour he was still lonely. The car was awesome, yet it was no fun with out Jenny.

Back at his apartment Harold sat in silence for a long time, thinking about Jenny and how she just flipped out on him. He figured since she wouldn't take any of his calls that maybe he should write her a letter:

My dearest Jenny

I am writing you this letter because you never gave me a chance to explain myself. I don't understand where you got the idea that I am still married. I don't have a wife. I am enclosing a copy of my actual divorce papers to prove to you my honesty and sincerity. Jenny I am madly in love with you and I have not been able to get you off my mind.

If you receive this letter, please let me know because I would like to see you one more time. I need closure. We cannot end this like this, I haven't done anything wrong.

I LOVE YOU JENNY.

From the bottom of my heart,

Harold.

Harold signed the letter then opened his kitchen drawer and threw everything on the floor until he found the envelope containing his divorce papers. He placed the letter along with his divorce papers inside the envelope and sealed it throwing it upon the kitchen table to be mailed out the next day.

Chapter Thirteen

"LET ME IN you can't throw me out! I have nowhere to go Carl, please open this door," Linda yelled.

Carl opened the door with fury. "You're a lousy ho! I can't believe you were on my bed with that piece of shit."

"Listen Carl please, just let me in so I can explain," she begged.

"Explain what? I should have known what kind of woman you were. You left your first husband so we could get married. What do you want from me?" Carl screamed.

"Please let me come in and I can explain. I want to help you."

"What do you mean help me?"

"Move out of the way my son is all wet," Linda said as she pushed her way into the house.

She quickly undressed Jonathan and began drying him with a towel.

"Carl listen," she started. "You are in a bad financial situation. Our co-op is foreclosing and you lost your job.

We need money actually bad and Harold has a business. The bagel shop is a very good business as a matter of fact. I sit there and watch tons of people go in and out every day," she said redressing her son.

"What does that have to do with me?" Carl asked.

"Well if I can get Harold back and win over his heart one more time, then I can work my way into becoming partners in his business and take control of it. But in the meantime you have to play it cool and act like you don't have a clue. Harold is stupid he won't realize a thing."

"I do not know about this. What if you leave me for someone else after you get his money?"

"I would never leave you," Linda said sitting her son in a booster seat.

Slowly she walked toward Carl unbuttoning her wet shirt and pulling her bra down. She slowing began touching her pink nipple. Linda pressed herself onto Carl's body grabbing a hold of his manhood, holding it until it hardened.

"You have more to offer me than Harold. He is just a wimp who I am using for his money. Trust me I won't leave you out. Whatever I do you gotta back me up though." Linda kissed Carl on his neck and licked behind his ears as she made him melt with her seducing tactics.

"Okay Linda, you got a deal, but if you lie to me I'll kill both of you. I promise," Carl said grabbing her body closer to his.

"Trust me." She grabbed his hand and placed it on her breast.

Linda dragged Carl on the living room floor and had ruthless sex.

Harold went to the post office to mail his letter to Jenny when he read a notice posted on a wall for free puppies. Harold called the number and a woman answered the phone. She gave him her address and after he left the post office he headed to her home.

At the elderly woman's home, she introduced him to a beautiful golden retriever nestled next to six golden puppies.

"I would keep them all but it would be too much for me," she explained.

Harold lifted one up and it smiled. It had big brown eyes with white paws.

"Can I have this one?" Harold asked, never taking his eyes off the puppy.

"You sure can, she's a cutie."

"Thank you very much,"

"I have had her mother Tessi about six years now and she is my best friend."

"This little one is going to be in good hands." He smiled.

Harold felt like a child on Christmas day as his heart raced with exhilaration. The puppy sat on his lap as he drove to a nearby pet shop. Harold held the puppy in his arms like a proud father as he walked into the pet shop. Two women employees immediately walked over to him and began ooo'ing and ahhh'ing over his new roommate.

"Does she have a name?"

"I just got her, I haven't thought of one yet," Harold said.

"You should call her Dolly she looks like a little doll," one woman remarked.

"Dolly," Harold repeated. "I like that."

Harold held the puppy up to his face and she licked his nose with her tiny warm tongue.

"I need your help," he said. "Give me everything I need for her from bed to toys and food."

The two women ran around the store picking up toys and food and Harold ended up spending over two hundred dollars in the pet shop.

When he arrived home, he pictured how delighted Jenny would be to see Dolly because she always wanted a dog. He decided he would give her a call within a week so she could have time to read the letter. Hopefully, she'd call him before then. She had to once she found out the truth and saw the divorce papers with her own eyes.

Jenny had heat exhaustion she could no longer stay in the sun following her prop around making sure it didn't fall apart. She advised Stefan to take over as she walked back to the hotel for some relief from the unforgiving heat.

It was very cool in her room and she relaxed a little and ordered room service. A knock came at the door and Jenny peeked to the hole to find Mouhab standing in the hallway holding a big bouquet of flowers.

"Open up I know you are there," he said.

Jenny hesitated for a moment then opened the door letting him in the room.

"These are for you," he said holding the roses out for her to take. "I came to apologize for my behavior."

Jenny began to sneeze uncontrollably. "I'm allergic to those flowers for some reason."

"Oh my I am so sorry Jenny, wait I will leave them here," he laid them on the floor in the hallway. "Please let me come in I won't touch you."

Jenny opened the door wider and he slid by her.

"Are you alright now?" he asked

"Yes thank you." Jenny was very nervous about having him in the room. She started to think she had made a huge mistake.

"I only want to be your friend. How long have you worked with Dlite Inc.?"

"About five years," she said moving to the sofa.

Mouhab remained standing near the door.

"Your creature looks almost real it scares me, those fangs are disgusting. You've done amazing work."

"Thank you, I actually had help from a friend," Jenny said, thinking about Harold.

"Well both of you did a great job. So do you accept my apology?"

"Yes I only hope it will not happen again."

"I won't touch you ever again, actually I want to invite you to dancing in the lounge. I usually host a band on Friday nights."

"Maybe I will, I'm getting homesick and could use a distraction."

"Well come to the party tonight, it will definitely get your mind off of things."

"Thank you and I do accept your apology."

The sheik smiled. "I'll see you tonight."

After he left Jenny took a nap since she was going to stay up all night at the party.

Chapter Fourteen

HAROLD SPRAYED COLOGNE on. He was getting ready for a date with a woman who replied to his profile on Love.com. After dressing he rushed out the door so he could be at the park on time.

Harold sat patiently on a bench. He watched all the couples holding hands and wondered how some people could be so lucky to have these long lasting relationships.

Some one tapped him on the shoulder so Harold turned around. A woman smiled at him, she had blond hair and was short and chubby. Not exactly, Harold's type however he tried to make the best of it.

"Hello Harold," she said with a high-pitched squeaky voice. Her tiny annoying voice definitely didn't match her huge frame.

"Hi Nancy," Harold said uncertain.

"Yes it's me. It's nice to meet you," she said.

Harold's ears began to ache at the sound of her voice.

"Harold I want to ask you why you wanted to meet at the park, I found this very strange."

"I did not want to leave my puppy Dolly home alone I needed to be somewhere she could come also."

"Where is she?"

"Here." Harold opened up his jacket and Dolly stuck her head out.

"Wow! She's adorable!" Nancy screeched loudly.

Harold got up from the bench to quiet her down. Her sound was worse than his car alarm.

"Okay let's take a walk," Harold said letting Dolly get down as he held her leash.

"It's a beautiful fall day I love this time of year," Nancy said.

"Yes it is nice although the holidays are coming soon and it's a very depressing time of year for me."

"I'm sorry to hear that Harry. Is it okay for me to call you that?"

Harold was annoyed; however he didn't stop her because he just wanted to this date to be over with since he felt a migraine coming.

"OOOOH look the hot dog vender," she said again in her irritating tone. "Let's go get one."

"Okay, sounds good." Harold walked quickly to catch up with Nancy who was already half way there.

"Do you know how long it's been since I've had one of these?" Nancy asked biting into the hot dog smearing ketchup and mustard on the sides of her mouth.

Harold tried to hide the disgusted look on his face.

"Would you like one sir?" the vendor asked.

"No, I suddenly lost my appetite," Harold said trying to figure out a way to end the date.

"Harold let's go to my place I want to show you my dog. Dolly will love him," Nancy said with a mouth full of food.

"I really can't," he started. "I need to get back home; I have a lot of work to do."

"Please, please," Nancy said pulling Harold by the hand like a five year old child.

"Alright I will come see your dog I guess Dolly needs a friend to play with. But I can't stay long."

"You are going to love Checkers," Nancy said lifting Dolly towards her face.

"Okay only for a couple of minutes."

Harold entered Nancy's apartment walked into the kitchen and sat down at the table. Nancy offered Harold a glass of water. Harold placed Dolly on the soft carpet; the puppy slowly walked over and drank some water from a drinking bowl.

"Checkers come here boy," Nancy called out.

Suddenly an enormous longhaired gray white Old English sheepdog came running out of the bedroom. The large dog had saliva dripping out of his mouth as he jumped on Harold licking his face and knocking him down to the ground. The dog continued to lick his face as Harold fought in vain to get the dog off him.

Nancy ran over grabbing Checkers by the collar pulling him off Harold dragging the dog into one of the bedrooms shutting the door behind her.

"I'm so sorry," Nancy said through giggles.

Harold's face was slimy he immediately ran to the restroom to wash his face once he got directions from Nancy.

"I am sorry Harold he gets excited when we have company."

Harold emerged from the bathroom wiping his face with a towel. "I have to get going I'm late for work."

"I didn't know you worked today you didn't mention that."

"Yeah I work in the evenings." Harold picked up Dolly and tucked her safely in his arms.

Checkers continued to bark ferociously from the other side of the closed bedroom door.

Harold made his way toward the door. "Well it was nice meeting you thanks for the water."

"Yes Harold nice meeting you I will see you around," Nancy said.

Harold looked down at Dolly and realized once again, it was just she and he.

Chapter Fifteen

HAROLD OVERSLEPT AND Debra had to open up by herself. The morning rush was about to start and she was feeling a little overwhelmed.

Linda walked through the front door, "Hello is Harold here?" Linda said looking irritated.

Debra turned slowly to face Linda.

"He should be here any minute," Debra, said keeping her back to Linda.

"Give me some coffee!" Linda demanded.

Debra slowly made the cup of coffee as she quietly cussed Linda under her breath.

"One dollar and fifty cents," Debra said.

Linda rolled her eyes. "I do not pay in here."

Harold walked through the door and was surprised to see Linda.

"Hello Linda, what are you doing here?"

"Hi Harold, how are you doing?"

"Is every thing alright?" Harold asked.

"Everything is fine."

Debra walked into the room. "Good morning Harold," she said hoping he would get rid of Linda.

"Hey Deb, good morning."

"Harry I need to talk to you," Linda said rubbing Harold's shoulder.

"What?" Harold said walking with Linda to an empty table.

"I have been thinking about you lately. I can't get you off my mind," she said seducing him with her eyes.

"Linda I don't know what you want me to say."

Linda moved closer to him and wrapped her arms around his waist.

"Linda I really don't think it can work."

"Why not?" She pressed herself against him tighter.

"I need time, you can't just decide you want me back this way," Harold insisted.

"Do you think of me? Do you miss me at all?"

"Linda I can't deal with this right now."

"What do you mean?"

Harold shook his head. "I'm living a different life right now and you can't come in here and complicate things even more." Harold grabbed her wrists removing her hands from him.

"Please then do me a favor I need a job," Linda begged.

"You need a job?"

"Yes, a job. Our co-op is about to be foreclosed on. Carl is not working. We really need the money," Linda said sounding desperate.

Harold felt guilty about her situation. "Actually I could use the help, the shop is getting very busy," Harold said.

"So I can work here?" Linda asked innocently.

"I guess so; let me get Debra to show you around."

Linda stood back and smiled as Harold went to talk to Debra.

"Deb, Linda is our new employee I need you to show her what to do."

"You're joking right?" Debra said sarcastically.

"No I'm not. She needs work and we need the help."

"I refuse to work with her," Debra protested.

"Deb, what is the problem?"

"Harold if she works here I quit."

"Come on you have been complaining that you need help."

"Harold I am serious I can't stand that woman."

"She has issues," Linda snapped at Debra

"Alright Debra if you will be uncomfortable then I won't hire her."

"Harold!" Linda said grabbing Harold by the arm.

"I am sorry Linda but I need Debra, she runs my business better than I do at times."

"I can do the same if you would just trust me," she whined.

Harold walked out the door with Linda. "Listen I'll try to convince Debra do not worry. I'll call you."

"You know I can do a better job. Harold you have known me for over ten years you should be able to trust me with your business."

"I don't think so. I trusted you too much and you let me down."

Customers were starting to pile into the shop. "I got to go Linda I'll call you," Harold said as he turned around and walked back through the door past the counter through the back doors of the store.

Jenny walked around the room with an apple martini in her hand. She watched all her co-workers laughing and having a good time.

Jenny never mingled with any of them since they were all happily married with children. She sat down at a table next to Stefan since he was the only one who acknowledged her.

"Having fun?" he asked sarcastically. "Just one more week then we get to go home," Stefan said.

"I know," Jenny sounded pitiful

"Jenny you are such a beautiful girl with a lonely heart," Stefan said.

"Unfortunately I have not had the luck that all of you have had," she said raising her glass as a sign of cheer.

"You want to talk about it?"

"What can I say? I fell for the wrong man."

"What was so wrong about him?"

"He's a cheater and a liar."

"Wow, and you're sure about this?"

Jenny raised her eyebrows at Stefan's comment. "Yes I am. He's just like every other man."

"Not every man cheats," Stefan protested.

"How long have you been married?'

"Thirty years."

"So you are telling me that you have been faithful for thirty years?"

"Yes I am," he said confidently.

"I don't believe it."

"Jenny if you don't believe that a man can possibly fall in love then don't bother."

"What do you mean?"

"When you fall in love do you consider cheating?"

"No not at all."

"Then why should a man? Only men who are not fully in love cheat."

"I hope you are right as for me I have yet to find that man."

"You have to truly believe in some one and most importantly believe in yourself."

Suddenly Mouhab grabbed Jenny and dragged her to the dance floor.

"Show me some of your American dancing."

"I don't know any I have not danced in a long time."

The live band at the hotel played old Elton John music as Mouhab twirled the five foot six, slim Jenny around the room.

"You are dancing like a professional," Jenny commented.

Jenny let herself go, she began to move her body freely. The music entered her system and she danced the night away trying to keep Harold out of her mind.

Chapter Sixteen

HAROLD WAS WRAPPING up a very busy night. Debra had gone home while Harold cleaned up and closed up the shop. He opened his register to count his earnings. Suddenly a knock came at the door. He walked over and did not see any one so he turned to walk away. Again, some one knocked. Harold opened the door to see who could be outside. A tall man dressed in black with a baseball hat, sunglasses and a handkerchief tied around his mouth suddenly pushed Harold inside, punched him in the face knocking Harold unconscious to the ground.

Moments later Harold regained consciousness and his face was throbbing in pain. He walked over and noticed the register was empty and became furious. The police arrived immediately. The police insisted that he go to a hospital but Harold refused. After the cops left he drove straight to Debra's house.

"Harold what happened?"

"I was robbed at the bagel shop."

"Oh my God! Are you okay?" Debra walked over to the fridge and pulled out some ice cubes and dumped them in a plastic bag for Harold's eye.

"Thanks," he said. "I can not believe it!"

"Who would've done something like this?"

"Obviously someone who desperately needed money," Harold said.

"Maybe someone who noticed how busy we were."

"What are you talking about?"

"Never mind, keep the ice pack on your eye."

"Debra, do you mind if I stay here tonight?"

She pointed, "Of course not there is a spare bedroom down that hallway."

"Thanks," Harold slowly walked towards the bedroom.

He desperately needed to hear Jenny's voice. He dialed her home number and her answering machine picked up. He also tried her cell phone, but again there was no answer. He laid his head on the pillow and fell asleep.

Linda caressed Carl's hair as he counted the money.

"Three thousand two hundred eighty five dollars," Carl said with joy.

"Awesome you can pay the bills and get us back on the track," Linda said massaging Carl's huge muscular back.

She wore a silk black nightgown; her breasts fully round were rubbing against Carl. Carl excitedly ran his fingers through Harold's hard-earned money.

"I love this idea you are brilliant," Carl said turning to kiss Linda.

"That moron doesn't know what a gold mine he has," Linda commented.

"Linda I can do this once a week."

"No do not push it, we could get discovered. Let's wait a couple of months, the police are probably investigating."

"Police do not investigate small robberies. Plus they have no witnesses or a description."

"Trust me just wait. I am going to get that job in there and then it will be a piece of cake."

"You're a genius," Carl said. He tossed the money up in the air and began kissing Linda.

They had sex as the money fell on top of their naked bodies.

"Linda do what you have to do, we need his money."

"Are you saying I can sleep with him?" Linda said as she walked naked into the bathroom.

"I hate the idea but if it works it'll save me from getting a job."

"You need to get a job this money will not keep us for that long."

"You're my bitch," Carl said as he walked into the bathroom smacking Linda on her rear.

"Don't call me a bitch; I'll take my money back."

"Your money? That'll happen over my dead body. I put my life on the line for this," Carl said as he picked up the money from the floor.

Linda slipped her nightgown over her head and put on her high heel shoes. She walked over and stepped on Carl's hand.

"Ouch what are you doing?" Carl said. His hand ached as the thin heel dug deep into his skin.

"I am not your bitch Carl. Don't you dare call me that again." She bent down picked up a hand full of money and walked out the room.

Carl held his hand shaking his head at the sexy feisty woman he dearly cared for.

Pointing at her he stated, "You know if I did not love you so much I would smack the hell out you. One of these days it just might happen."

Linda laughed and started playing with the stiletto on her right foot. "A good fight makes for good love making after. Don't you think?"

Carl shook his head in disbelief. "You're crazy!"

Chapter Seventeen

JENNY'S LAST DAY in Egypt finally arrived and she packed her clothes zippered her luggage and waited for service. A knock came at the door Jenny opened it dragging the suitcase assuming the bellhop arrived.

"Jenny I came over to say farewell it was a pleasure to have you here."

"My stay here was very comfortable everything was perfect."

"I am glad to hear that, I am sorry again for that terrible misunderstanding," Mouhab said as he grabbed her hand kissing it gently.

"We all make mistakes"

"Take my card if you ever come to Egypt come and visit me. Or better yet give me a call when you get home so I know you arrived safely."

Jenny placed the card in her pocket and a young man came to take her luggage downstairs.

"Take care Mouhab," Jenny said kissing him slightly on his cheek.

She threw her jacket over her shoulders and entered the van parked in front of the hotel.

"Hey there Jenny," Stefan said sitting next to her reading a newspaper.

"I did not recognize you," Jenny said turning to face him.

"You like my new hat?" Stefan asked. He was wearing a straw hat with leopard skin around it.

"Nice," Jenny laughed. "Very

"I know I should have bought one more Arabic or Egyptian, however I know my son will love it."

"That is sweet of you."

"Actually my son is paralyzed in a wheelchair."

"Oh wow."

"Yeah he has been that way since ten years old," Stefan said, sadness spreading across his face.

"What happened?"

"He was playing outside a car came speeding down the street crushed both legs."

"How old is he?"

"Twenty-five."

"Well he has a great father I am sure you give him courage."

"Sometimes I think he gives me courage... I love him so much."

The van drove off to the airport as Jenny stared out the window she realized her problems seemed small compared to other people. For this she was grateful.

Chapter Eighteen

"HAROLD I'M BEGGING you to keep that lady away from me. She can't stand me and I can't stand her. She's a female dog and you know it."

Harold tried to hug Debra but she turned, opened the door and walked inside the store leaving the door to shut behind her.

He wiped his forehead and ran his fingers through his hair.

"Debra, I know, I know but she needs help." He followed her inside. "Debra it's just going to be for a few months. Please, please help me out with this."

Debra crossed her arms and shot him a look that let him know she didn't want to hear it.

"All I know is she better not come in here trying to run things. I've been helping you all this time, not her remember that. When you were down sick to your stomach with her running out..."

"I know-I know," Harold cut in. "Lets forget about it, do what we have to do and get these few months out the way."

He walked behind the counter to Debra. "Listen, she is going to be here any minute now so lets make up. What do you say?" He held out his hand to her.

Her angry look quickly turned to a smile and she smacked his hand away, hugging him. Harold smiled, hugging her back tightly. The last thing he wanted was to have problems with the one person who stood by him when he was troubled the most.

"Deb you're my only true friend, I will never forget that."

The front door opened, followed by a slight breeze. "I'm here to start my first day," Linda announced.

Debra and Harold stared at each other. They both looked at Linda who was standing next to her husband who Harold remembered very well from the day he ran out the apartment.

Harold walked around the front counter banging his knee along the edge. The pain caused him to fall.

"Oh! Damn!" he yelled getting up and limping over to the two. Carl reached out and shook his hand. He didn't seem angry at all and this kind of surprised Harold considering the circumstances of their last encounter.

Carl spoke first. "Harold thanks for helping Linda and I out. Times have been tough and she really needs a job. You know with the baby and all and me not working. I have my pride but there are times when we have to think about what's the best thing to do. We need the money after all."

Harold smiled at Carl and then toward Linda who seemed to be really relaxed. "It's the least I can do."

Debra pretended to be working but she was listening to every word of their conversation. She took full inventory of Carl who stood a little over 6ft. and was slim. He's not bad looking she thought, in fact kind of attractive. But there was something about him, which caused an alarm to sound off in her head. She did not like him no matter how diplomatic he seemed through speaking. Linda's a slime ball, so there has to be something going on with him as well.

"Ok, hun I will pick you up at seven," Carl told Linda hugging and kissing her as Harold watched awkwardly.

Carl shook Harold's hand and walked out the door.

"Linda, you can work the register today. The item pricing is on the list on the right side of the counter. It's easy to figure out and you're smart so you will get it all in a day or two. Bagels are all the same price; it's just the toppings that make the amounts differ. The cookies are all the same, and so are the muffins, you just add ten cents for butter. The beverage prices are up on the board in back of you. And that's basically it."

He grabbed Linda by both shoulders firmly. "If you have any questions just ask Debra or me and we'll fill you in."

Both ladies looked at each other and Debra snorted and looked away, but Linda just smiled.

Harold was about to walk away when Linda said, "Harold thanks a lot I really appreciate the help."

"No problem. Now get to work." Harold walked out the front door limping a little.

Linda walked behind the counter and was greeted by Debra with a firm handshake.

"Now we meet on different terms. I hope you got out your system whatever was ailing you before because Harold does not need the headaches. And I worked hard to get this place together and running the way it is. And I'll be damned if you think you are going to come in here and start some shit!" Debra's face was red and her freckles stood out like goose bumps.

"I have a man, I just need a job for these few months. Harold is old news, remember I left him so you don't have to worry," Linda snorted. "What business is it of yours anyway? Your not Harold's type, he likes them hot and outgoing." Linda waved at her in a "whatever gesture." Before asking, "Where's the price lists?"

"Over there, by the register." Debra pointed. "And be ready Cinderella because the customers will start pouring in like 5 to 10 minutes. I have to bake so I don't have the time to baby-sit you."

Chapter Nineteen

JENNY'S FLIGHT ARRIVED at JFK airport at 8:00 p.m. As she waited in front of the terminal for a cab she reflected on the past few weeks and everything from Harold to Mahoub. A car horn blew jerking her from her thoughts.

"Ms. Are you waiting on a cab?"

Jenny snapped out the daze. "Yes! I'm sorry."

She held her hands to her face and began to laugh. "Oh my God it's been a crazy week. I have to get home," she said to no one in particular, just speaking loud.

The cabbie started placing her baggage in the trunk. "You can get in Ms. I will not forget anything."

His teeth were bright white and one of them was capped with white gold, which stood out in contrast to his dark smooth skin. Jenny smiled and nodded as she climbed into the cab. Once in the back seat she stretched out her legs yawning before resting comfortably all the way back, resting her neck into the cushion.

"Where are you going Ms?" he asked.

"4922 Green Avenue on the east side. Do you know the neighborhood?"

"Yes I do. It's the neighborhood with the brownstones. Very nice place."

He looked in the rearview mirror. "You look tired, rest up I know how to get there. We will be there before you know it; traffic is very light right now."

She looked ahead. "Thank you! I can't wait to get home."

Before she realized it the cab was right in front of her building. She had dozed off into a daydream about the past two weeks again, Harold, the trip and Mouhab.

"Okay, we are here."

When she came to the cabbie was outside the car, fumbling through the trunk for her belongings. He dragged them up the stairs to her door, jogging back to the car opening the door.

Getting out the car she asked, "How much do I owe you?"

"That will be six dollars." He held out the palm of his right hand.

Jenny reached into her right pocket pulling out one ten-dollar bill handing it to him. He looked from the bill to her and back to the bill in his hand.

"Do you want change Ms?"

"No, you can keep the change." Jenny smiled, turned away walking up the steps.

The car door slammed and the cab sped away screeching around the next corner.

Jenny fumbled through one of her luggage bags for the front door key, cursing, swearing and hoping she didn't lose them.

"Thank goodness!" she told herself when she found them.

Once in the apartment she walked over to the answering machine to check her messages. Eager to empty her bladder, she hit the button and the machine came to life replaying her messages. Walking to the bathroom she began to undress taking off her shirt top, and walking up out her pants. Her friends, Sandy and Caroline had left the first two messages. And then third message was Harold. He was swearing and promising this and that.

"Liar, liar pants on fire!" Jenny sang.

Third message was Harold, so was the fourth, fifth, sixth, seventh and eight.

She held her hands up to the air and then placed them upon her head. "Men, men why do we need them!"

By the time the seventh message kicked in she was in the shower with the sound of the water drowning out any possibilities of her hearing Harold state he had sent his divorce papers in the mail to her.

Jenny washed herself slowly taking in the warmth of the water and soap suds. She thought about Mouhab and how he'd turned out to be a nice guy after all. She decided she call him as soon as she got out to let him know she arrived ok.

"So sweet," she whispered.

She heard the phone ringing when she turned the shower off. With towel in hand she ran, drying herself off along the way to pick it up. The warm air hit her right away causing her to perspire from her body heat, and the warm water, which soaked her body. She almost tripped over the coach trying to reach the phone, but instead fell down upon it and reached over for the handle upon the fourth ring.

"Hello?"

"Oh! I was just checking to make sure you made it home. I was a little worried, because it is a long trip from Egypt."

"Mouhab, yes I'm ok. I was just about to call you. I just walked through the door about thirty minutes ago."

"Jenny, my dear I'm glad everything is fine. I have a surprise actually for us both. One of my colleagues has contacted me regarding a possible business arrangement in New York City. So I will be making a brief visit in two weeks. Maybe we can have lunch and I can make up for my rudeness back in Egypt. You know I'm actually a pretty nice guy."

Jenny's' face lit up with a smile. "That would be nice. Work lately has been driving me crazy."

Mouhab with confidence stated, "So now you have the perfect reason to be my chaperon."

Jenny stuttered, "Yeah-yeah, hmmm ok. But as long as you can behave yourself."

Mouhab started laughing. "You're a beautiful woman and I was just caught up in the moment," he said. "Jenny,

I'm just a man. Nothing more, nothing less so forgive me."

Jenny held the phone close to her ear with both hands. She could not hold back the urge to chuckle. "All is forgiven!"

"Well, then I will call within a week to confirm when I will be arriving. Go to rest, and sleep well Jenny."

Jenny sighed. "Good night Mouhab."

"Night, Jenny" Mouhab hung up first.

Jenny was so exhausted she didn't bother to look for pajamas. Instead she flung the towel to the bedroom floor and threw her naked body on the bed.

The warm breeze coming through the bedroom window felt good. Within a few minutes she was within a deep sleep and started to dream.

"Oh! Harold!"

"Jenny, my Jenny where have you been?"

"Oh, its been such a long day, I could not get the makeup right for this mask and then one of the actors was in rare form and had the director in an uproar so it was not the perfect day to say the least."

Harold grabbed a hold of her and started caressing her shoulders. Harold seemed so confident and sure of himself. It was just not like him. His hands were so warm and firm. Jenny moaned at every touch. She had not felt so good in such a long time. In fact she was totally lost within herself and had no sense of self-control. All she wanted and needed was to submerge her mind and body fully into how she was feeling. She did not care what happened just as long as it continued to escalate.

Harold was in full control, he took Jenny's shirt off and she did nothing to stop him or resist in anyway. Then he unbuttoned her bra, sliding the arm straps down along and off her arms. Holding her close to him from the back he began to kiss her neck. She moaned and was caught up in the warmth of his lips and the sweet sound of violins playing."

Just when she started to feel a tingling sensation between her thighs a voice came to her "Harold! Harold! Harold! I know you're in there!" Pounding at the door! "Harold! Harold! I'm going to kill you and that family wrecking whore!"

Drenched in sweat Jenny awoke "Jenny are you there? I have your mail, I'm a put it under the door."

Jenny recognized the voice of Ms. Johnson her neighbor who had agreed to pick up her mail while she was gone. Quickly she sat up, wiped the cold out her eye, rubbing her face finding it hard to believe it had all been a dream. She was feeling hot from head to toe and noticed right away she had cum. The inside of her thighs were wet with juices. Jenny blushed feeling a moment of embarrassment. Had it not been for the last part of the dream she would of really been upset that it was all just a dream.

"Harold, Harold this cannot happen." Right at this moment a thought of what to do came to her. She decided she'd change her phone number right away.

Getting out of bed she walked to the door picking up the mail. Uugghh it was all bills. Harold's letter was not in the pile because Ms. Johnson by accident placed the envelope inside an old newspaper, which she threw out a few days earlier.

After going through the bills Jenny called the phone company. Once this mission was accomplished she went to the shower to wash away the filth of it all. She vigorously scrubbed herself as if her body was covered in slime.

Chapter Twenty

"HAROLD PLEASE QUIT moping around."

"Debra, I'm trying but one minute my life is on the up and then the next minute I'm back to square one."

Harold picked up a muffin but dropped it once he realized it had just come out the oven.

"Damn! I burnt my hand."

Debra laughed. "Harold you have no luck with love and you're clumsy. What a combination."

"Shut up Deb."

Harold held his hands inside the sink under the cold running water. "I'm going to stop by Jenny's today. Hopefully she has gotten back from wherever she went. We need to fix this and make it right." Harold kept talking but Debra had walked up front to where Linda was at to help wipe off the tables and ready the store for the morning rush.

"I must be crazy," Harold said to himself. "I hired my ex-wife to work for me after she breaks up the best thing that has happened to me in a long a while."

Harold did not bother to dry off his hands; he walked to the front and out the door without uttering a word to anyone.

Linda was in the back and as she walked to the front she seen Harold walking out the front door cussing and swearing to himself.

Linda asked Debra, "What's gotten into Harold, he seems a bit uptight?"

Debra shot her a look. "You know having you around is enough to have anyone uptight."

Linda stopped wiping down her table and placed her hands on her hips. "You know you need to be a little nicer to me because sooner or later I will win my way back into Harold's heart and then you'll be gone if you don't fix that little attitude of yours."

Debra's face turned beet red and she couldn't hold back the anger or the urge to jump on Linda. She walked over to her just inches away so that their faces were close to one another.

"Now you listen to me you little heifer. Yeah you may have one up on Harold. But don't think he's dumb, he knows who you are. And as long as I'm around ain't anyone going to take advantage of him. So before I have to jump all over your ass one day I suggest you get your money together the next two weeks working here and then go on your way."

Just then the first customer of the day walked through the door. Both ladies looked once the bells chimed.

Debra walked behind the counter and looked at Linda. "We can continue this later."

"This is just the beginning of it, trust me," Linda whispered winking at Debra.

The customer noticed their subtle confrontation; he looked from one to the other before placing his order with Debra.

On the way to Jenny's house Harold's mind wandered to whether or not Jenny had actually read his divorce papers. He really wanted to clear all of this up so that they could get back to the way things were.

Screeching car tires snapped him out of his trance as the car ahead of him came to a screeching halt. Harold did not have time to think, pressing on the breaks he swerved to the right just making it around the car's bumper. Luckily no one was walking along the street or he would have hit them. He wiped the sweat from his brow and taking in a deep breath he looked in the rearview mirror before accelerating the car back onto the road. Like a student taking the drivers test he watched the road carefully all the way to Jenny's complex.

Getting out the car he closed the door and tripped on the curb. If he didn't extend his hands out in front he would have fell on his face. Jumping up back on his feet he looked around to see who was watching. He smirked, shaking his head relieved that no one was around to see one of his many clumsy episodes throughout a day.

His cell phone started to chime and vibrate in his pocket.

"Harold speaking!"

"What's up buddy it's me Mark. Nina asked me to call to see how everything is going with you."

"Well, I just tripped over the curb, Linda works for me now and I'm here at Jenny's place to see if we can fix things up. Other than this I live the perfect life. What would you say?"

"Harold you're the man you have it all together, the car, the business and you're gonna have your woman too. Just be patient, don't turn back into the old Harold. The one who needs to please everyone but himself. You know what I mean."

Harold nodded his head in agreement. "Yeah, yeah I know. But look who's talking. The guy who vowed to always be a player. Now you got Nina, your getting married and I'm here by myself. The car is nice. So is working for myself. But I'm just a regular guy deep down inside with old school values. All I want is to be happy and share it with the woman I love."

Harold stared ahead at Jenny's front door. "Let me go Mark, I need to talk with Jenny and fix this."

"Okay Harold, but if it doesn't work out remember the same way you met her you can meet someone else." Pausing for a moment he went on, "You're a ladies magnet now, nice car, self-employed. Just what they're looking for."

Mark started to laugh.

"Shut up! Let me go before I get scared and leave." Harold held the phone up to his face before speaking again. "Mark, I have to go. I need to make this right."

Harold hung up the phone and rang Jenny's doorbell. After not getting an answer, he rang the doorbell a second, third and fourth time. Beads of sweat began to pour down his forehead. In frustration Harold rang the doorbell a fifth time, holding it down for about ten seconds before letting go.

Harold stood up and momentarily was overcome by a dizzy spell. He shook his head from side to side and realized it was just the heat and the fact he was tired along with being stressed. He found his way back to the car and drove off. Approaching a red light he dialed Jenny's number.

"The number you've dialed has been disconnected. Please hang up and try again." He listened to the message only once but it echoed in his mind over and over.

As soon as Harold got home he walked straight to his office desk turning on the computer console.

"You got mail!" came through the speakers.

Harold anxiously clicked the inbox. There were 20 messages. Scrolling through all the spam mail he came across a new one from "Love.com" He sighed grabbing his forehead, contemplating a moment before clicking on the link.

He read the message quickly but was astounded by the pictures in the gallery.

"Wow!"

Hurriedly he went to the profile:

Name: Melissa

Age: 33yrs. old

Height: 5 '5'

Weight: 128lbs.

Ethnicity: Hispanic

He then started to read the message she sent him.

Hi,

My name is Melissa I read your profile and you seem like a very interesting guy. I'm not one to spend a lot of time with back and fourth emails so I would like to exchange numbers if this is ok with you. Mine is 000-232-0000. Please give me a call soon. I'm looking forward to talking to you.

Melissa.

Harold quickly went back to the photos. Her complexion turned him on. Not to mention the small waist and early 90's Jennifer Lopez buttocks. One picture was of her in a bikini bathing suit. Harold briefly contemplated downloading the pic and printing it so he could look at it often.

Harold whispered "Melissa, Melissa" resting his head upon the desks counter and closing his eyes. Quickly he dozed off, snoring heavily.

Jenny walked through the door and the phone started ringing. Dropping the bags upon the welcome mat she ran to pick it up.

"Jenny who's speaking?"

"Ahh-Jenny it's me Mouhab I will be leaving this afternoon for New York. I was hoping we could meet for lunch this weekend."

Jenny started laughing. "Mouhab, it's already Friday. The weekend starts tomorrow or tonight whichever is best for the individual." Exhaling she ran her fingers through her hair. "The weekend is fine. What hotel you'll be staying in?"

"Ahh, I believe the Sheraton. But either way my associates have this all arranged for me. I will be picked up from John F. Kennedy and driven to where I'll be staying." He started laughing- "I'm going to need to rest a bit after this flight. Every time I come to New York there are always some very interesting passengers. I'll probably be checked and screened ten times getting off the flight. You know us Arabs are all assumed to be terrorists. This is especially so here in NYC."

"Ha-ha-ha Mouhab, please don't say that. It's not that bad! Here in the states there are all types of stereotypes, white, black, fat, skinny the list goes on."

"Hmm ok Jenny my dear. I must ready myself for the trip. I will call you tomorrow after I've rested up."

"Mouhab I'm looking forward to seeing you again."

Jenny hung up and smiled. She figured it might be easier to get over Harold than she originally thought.

Chapter Twenty-One

THE DRIVER CALLED out "Watch your step Miss." At least this is what Jenny thought because it was kind of hard to decipher exactly what was said because his pronunciation was very poor. She figured his accent to be Haitian or African.

Jenny walked down the stoop past the driver to Mouhab. Once they reached one another he took her hand in his and gently hugged her.

"Jenny my dear it's a pleasure to see you."

Jenny smiled. "Mouhab thank you." She stopped to look him up and down. "That suit looks very nice on you; it does a lot for your olive complexion."

He squeezed her hand. "Ah, my dear the compliment is welcomed. Let us go, I have a reservation for us set. We need to be there within twenty minutes."

Mouhab helped Jenny into the back seat. The driver closed the door and stepped in behind the wheel. He wiped at the sweat, which was forming, along his forehead.

As they drove Mouhab stared ahead at the scenery on the other side of the windshield. Jenny eyed him, thinking how handsome he was. She also liked the fact he had no facial hair other than his close-cropped mustache. She didn't know how, but he suddenly turned her on.

Mouhab turned toward Jenny and smiled and for a few seconds said nothing.

"Jenny."

Jenny's face lit up. "Yes!"

"I just want you to know that I'm truly sorry about the way I acted on your visit to Egypt. You're a beautiful woman and your beauty and my loneliness overcame me. My wife died in a car crash three years ago and I've been single and miserable. I just wanted to live again." He fixed his suit, pulling on the front. "Can you understand this?"

Jenny had stars in her eyes. "Mouhab, I told you before I accept your apology. And I'm sorry to hear about your wife's death."

He once again grabbed a hold of her hand. "Thank you for meeting me."

The driver looked in the rearview mirror. He smiled and his teeth glistened.

Mouhab took his eyes off Jenny to look ahead. "Driver you can drop us off in the front of the restaurant."

The driver nodded.

Jenny was feeling good and her face was glowing as she still held hands with Mouhab.

The car pulled over to the curb and the driver let them out. The restaurant was Italian, and there were a lot of sculptures and paintings all around the fancy scenery. The waiter spoke with a very heavy accent and Jenny found it hard to understand him at all. Mouhab ordered for them both surprising Jenny that he was fluent in Italian as well.

After Mouhab ordered she whispered, "Mouhab I'm glad you can speak Italian because I haven't the slightest idea what he is saying. His English is so poor!"

Mouhab laughed, "Jenny my dear I'm so sorry but I was told they make good food here." He put both hands in the air and started laughing before saying "Maybe since you're from here I should have let you make dinner arrangements."

"Mouhab, hush! Let's just make the best of it because it could be worse."

He stared into her eyes and they both smiled. Right at that moment the house band began playing. A few minutes later the waiter came pushing a food cart placing their dinner upon the table. They ate and drank before dancing into the late hours of the night.

The next morning Jenny awoke with Mouhab lying next to her. She looked over to him, snuggling close and tried to remember how it all happened. From side to side she shook her head and laughed.

Mouhab sighed and started to wake.

"It's nothing. Go back to sleep" she told him before lying on her back and stretching out. For a brief second Harold crossed her mind.

Harold walked through the front door of the bagel shop whistling and bopping his head from side to side. Linda and Debra are cleaning tables. "Hi ladies. Good morning!"

They both look up toward him startled.

Linda asks, "What has you so cheery Harold? Yesterday you seemed a bit upset. I hope everything is alright." She added the last sentence with emphasis, sneaking a peak toward Debra who was staring her way, angry faced with both hands upon her hips.

"Everything is fine. I have a lunch date this afternoon. And man, I'm looking forward to it. It's just what I need right now." Harold clapped his hands together, rubbing both palms, cracking his knuckles. "Just what I need." He smiled and walked to the back of the store bumping his head into the door.

Linda momentarily watched his back. Debra eyed her closely and started to laugh once Harold disappeared through the back door.

Linda scowled. "What are you laughing about?"

Debra smirked and sniffed. "You little heifer. I'm glad he has a date. Now you can get it out of your head that you and Harold will ever get back together." She began to wipe down the table again. "Get over it, you left him and it took him a while, but he's over you. And thank God!"

"Oh! Shut up. Harold's a grown man; you'll never know him like I do. He'll always love me. What you need to do is find yourself a man and stop worrying about Harold."

Debra dropped the cloth to the floor and walked hurriedly to the other woman. Just as Linda was about to open her mouth and say something Debra smacked her across the face sending her sprawling into a table. She fell flat on her back. Saliva and blood foamed around her lips. Her face turned a beat red.

She yelled, "You crazy bitch!"

Linda was up on her feet immediately. She was ready for the fight and angry at seeing her own blood. Like an experienced boxer, with fists she rushed Debra who stood in counter defense mode. Linda punched Debra just above the breasts and Debra smacked her again before they both locked onto one another, wrestling and scratching each other to the wooden floor.

"You bitch!"

"You slut!"

All types of obscenities were screamed out as they tussled.

Harold ran from the back. "What the hell is going on?"

He pried them away from one another and by accident Debra smacked him causing his head to jerk back from the impact.

He looked toward her. "Now beat me up why don't you."

Linda ran to the back crying, sniffling and holding her cherry red face. Debra fixed herself and walked out the front door.

"Where are you going?" Harold kept asking following her out the door.

She answered him on his fourth time. "I'll be back. Go check on your little princess. She might have a broken nail and some bruises."

Harold ran both hands through his hair. "Great! This is great! Now I have to deal with this." He looked up to the sky. "God why me? Why me?"

The last thing he wanted was for a customer to come. As he walked toward the back he could hear Linda weeping and his heart began to melt. They may have been separated but he still loved her.

As soon as Harold stepped through the back door he saw Linda balled into a fetus position near the dishwasher. Concerned he walks over to her, hugging her tightly.

"Linda what happened?"

Linda reached at him, smacking him in the chest. "It's you. It's your fault. I got jealous. I can't help it, I just can't help it." She looked up toward him. Her eyes were bloodshot red and watery from crying and Debra's handprint was on the side of her face.

Harold said nothing, for a few moments they stared into each other's eyes. Just when Harold was going to pull away Linda reached out grabbing him.

He tried to push her off. "No! No! No Linda! This can't happen." He even placed both hands upon her face telling her, "This can't happen!"

She reached for his belt buckle holding his pants line tight as he tried to pull away from her. "I don't care that we are not together. I need you right now; I want you to want me. If anything at least just for right now."

Linda proceeded to go down on Harold. "How did it come to this?" he began to wonder. She handled him rough with a hunger that turned him on. She got up, pulled up her dress and stood up against the dishwasher. He hated her for all she did to him, but he also lusted for her. With animalistic passion he began to thrust in and out of her. Pulling her hair from the back and squeezing her by the waist tightly. They both talked to each other dirty, calling each other names, swearing and cursing at one another. Sweat dripped from both of their bodies and their body heat made the room feel like it was on fire.

The front door buzzer rung and on the third ring Harold came to, realizing that it must be Debra at the front door. Or even worse it might be a customer.

Harold pulled away from Linda, slipped up his boxers, then pants. He wiped his face, fixed his shirt and noticed that the front was wet with perspiration. "Shit!!"

Walking to the front he exhaled seeing that it was only Debra instead of a customer. He wondered if she could see his guilt through the door and decided that he would open the door, let her in and keep walking to his car.

He opened the door. "Harold why was the door locked?"

Harold said nothing; he just walked past her saying, "I don't want no more fighting today. I'm going home to get some rest and prepare for my date. Close up and I'll see you both tomorrow."

Debra yelled, "But—"

Harold disappeared around the corner and didn't look back.

She was suspicious because Harold never acted like this with her. Hurriedly she walked to the back to see what Linda was up to. Stepping through the back door both of their eyes locked upon one another. Linda was fixing her dress. She was sweaty and wore a sick looking smirk. There was something sinister to her grin Debra thought. Without saying anything Debra shook her head, sucked her teeth, exhaling and walked back to the front.

Linda started to laugh.

Chapter Twenty-Two

THE PHONE RINGING woke Harold. Wiping the sleep out his eyes and yawning he picked it up letting the handset fall to the bed before answering it.

With closed eyes he spoke, "Hello?"

"It's me Mark. Where the hell have you been? We need to go out, have some drinks and laugh it up like old times. I'm going to be married soon so I—"

Harold started laughing into the handset. "Don't tell me you're now getting nervous Mark. Mr. Cool, the guy who has it all together. Man, don't worry it will be a breeze. It will be just like a dream. You marry the woman of your dreams. She is perfect and everything that you want. Then as time goes by you both start to change, maybe your love grows stronger. Maybe she turns into another Linda."

He started laughing again.

"Mark, I'm going on a date later with this very hot Latin woman. I don't know what she saw in my profile, but I can tell you I think she is a work of art. She has a body that I never seen on a woman before. I thought

Linda was hot in her earlier years." Pausing for a second he continued. "Speaking of Linda, today I did her in the bagel shop. I didn't want to but she came on to me and my emotions got the best of me. For once in my life I wanted to have control over her. She wanted me, and I hate her so, but lusted for her at the same time so I gave it to her like a crazy mad man!"

Mark was startled. "What! Man, Harold you are getting crazy! I think all this stuff is really starting to get to you. The break up with Linda, and then Jenny has got you going nuts. You have to calm down. I don't know maybe you shouldn't go on this date. Maybe you should just try to get back with Jenny."

Harold was fully awake now. "You're the one who told me to forget about her and that just as easy as I found her I could find another woman. And that's what I did."

Harold started laughing again. "I think you're the one who is losing it. One minute you're telling me to live it up and then the next you're telling me to go back to being the old Harold who was a good guy who no one respected." Harold stopped talking for a breath minute. Neither of them spoke before he continued in a soft tone. "Mark, good guys end up last. I can't be the doormat anymore. I just can't do it. I'll call you tomorrow."

Harold hung up the phone before Mark could protest. He lied awake in bed for a few minutes before taking a shower. Even though he had his clothes out and ready since yesterday he wondered if what he picked would be appropriate. He laid the shirt and pair of slacks across the bed and stared. "Why not?" he told himself and began to dress.

The phone rang as he was putting on the slacks. With one leg in the pants he tried to run to the phone but slipped and fell, pulling the phone off the counter onto the floor. He screamed out, "Oh damn!" and picked it up.

"Hello."

"Are you ok? I heard you scream what happened?"

Harold was embarrassed as he felt his face turn red. "I'm, I'm ok. I was just walking to the phone and had a little accident. That's all nothing much."

Maria started to laugh, "Don't worry Papi, I will take good care of you. Hopefully you are ready for me."

Harold's face lit up with a smile. "I will be there to pick you up at 1 P.M. sharp. Are you ready?"

With perfect English she stated, "Of course, I'm just curling my hair."

"Maria can I ask you a question?"

"Of course baby."

"I wanted to know how is it that you speak very good English. I mean you hardly have an accent. I don't know, maybe its dumb question to ask."

"No! It's ok. I get asked that question all the time. Well, my parents are from Puerto Rico, but I was born here in New York and learned English and Spanish as a kid. My father only spoke Spanish in the house. My mother wanted me to learn English so she wouldn't speak

Spanish to me, only English." Laughing she continued. "So, I'm what you call a New York Rican."

Harold   chuckled.   "Oh!   All   right.   That's understandable."

"Well, let me finish doing my hair babe because it's a little after twelve and if we stay on the phone this date will not happen. Bye!"

"Bye!"

"Don't be late Harold!" Maria added.

Harold chuckled. "Ok, I won't I promise."

As soon as he hung up he rushed like a mad man to do everything he needed to do. He was glad he had gotten a hair cut the previous day because all he had to do was throw some after shave on his face and brush his hair once over and it was all good to go.

At 12:20 p.m. he was walking out the door to the car. The Mercedes sparkled and he took quick inventory of how the silver glistened from the waxing it had gotten last week. Getting in on the passengers side he revved up the engine and took it into drive.

Maria lived in an apartment complex on 164th & Jamaica Avenue. Knowing this he realized it would be better if he parked a few blocks away and walked over to her building because 164th was a one way street.

After maneuvering in and out of the heavy traffic and double parked cars he came around to her block. She was standing near the curb just out in front of the building. Harold was so mesmerized by her that he almost drove into the back of a car, which had come to a stop. Quickly he brought the car to a screeching halt almost banging his head on the dashboard because he wore no seatbelt.

Maria recognized the car from Harold's picture gallery on *Love.com* and quickly walked over. She wore a pair of tight fitting jeans, a half top and pair of white tennis sneakers. She looked even more beautiful in person than her pictures did on the Internet.

Harold stopped the car looking over his shoulder nervously at the car in back of him. Quickly Maria got in and kissed him on the cheek, reached over and wiped the lipstick off his face.

Maria asked, "So where are we off to?"

"Hmmm. I guess to find somewhere to eat."

Harold was a bit nervous and fidgeted a little. His hands shook a little on the steering wheel. Maria looked out in front of the windshield and out toward the sides. She watched all the people going to and from their destinations and smiled all the while. Harold on the contrary was finding it hard to settle in. He felt clumsier than ever and was at a loss for words. He just drove.

Maria pointed. "Harold I know a nice Indian restaurant just around the block. Let's go there because I love their curry chicken. Plus, it's a nice cozy place." She touched his arm gently. "We can talk there without too much distraction."

"Oh, ok. Do I turn here? Or the next block."

Maria pointed ahead. "Make a right on the next block, and then you can park the car in the first parking lot on the right. They charge but it's safer than leaving it on the street. These parking meter cops are all over the place and they do not care if you are one second over your time. They live to give a ticket out believe me." She started to laugh.

Harold smirked replying, "I don't need anymore tickets, I have quite a few already. It's a wonder how my license has not gotten suspended yet."

Maria started to laugh. "Harold you're so crazy and down to earth. We're going to have such a good time today."

The parking lot was half full, and they both were glad there was room left to park. After parking they walked across the street over to the restaurant. Harold opened the door for Maria and as he followed her in he tripped almost falling on his face. "Whoa! Whoa!" he yelled out catching his balance.

Maria began laughing uncontrollably before grabbing a hold of his arm.

A hostess came over to them and asked if they needed a table for two.

Maria replied. "Yes and the back will be fine." Still holding Harold's arm in hers she smiled at him. "It's nice and cool in here and the back is real cozy." She sucked her teeth. "And the food is delicious."

Harold was not embarrassed anymore but he was feeling a bit self-conscious. He kept looking around and about the restaurant, not making too much eye contact with Maria as she freely spoke to him as if they'd known each other for a long while.

Once seated Harold slumped over a bit taking in the cool air of the air-conditioned atmosphere. It felt so good. "It does feel good in here Maria."

"I told you this is a very nice place. And it's not crowded around this time, which makes it even better. I come here sometimes during lunch break at least twice a week." Looking around she continued. "In fact I'm surprised some of my co-workers are not here now. They probably went to the diner around the avenue because there is also a pretty good diner in the area where you serve yourself just like a Chinese buffet."

Harold could not help but stare at Maria's breasts. She wore a bra under the thin fabric but the top of her breasts stood out a little over the top of the bra lining. Maria noticed Harold staring but didn't say anything.

The waiter came asked them for their order and disappeared back into the kitchen. Maria excused herself to the bathroom and Harold found himself staring at her backside as she walked away.

He whistled to himself at the sight.

A moment later his cell phone went off. He looked at the number, realizing it was Mark.

"What Mark?"

"I was just checking up on you to see how things were going. Nina wanted me to call to make sure things were ok with you. I told her about our conversation and she was a bit worried. She wants to know if you want to come by for dinner tonight. And-"

"Mark what are you doing? You're lucky she went to the bathroom. She-"

"Harold how does she look? Is she hot?"

"Man, Mark she is more than hot. If I look at her in her face to talk I find myself staring at her breasts. She just left to go to the bathroom, and I could not help but to stare at her butt as she walked all the way there. If you had not called me right now I'd probably be daydreaming about her right now." He chuckled "Some type of friend you are disturbing my day dreams."

"Sounds like my old days. Does she have a boyfriend, married anything like that. A lady who looks like you describe more often than not has some guy. Even if she doesn't you have to be careful with the jealous ex. I've been down that road many times, and Harold they are some crazy fuckers, especially with hot chic's like that."

Harold could see Maria walk through the bathroom door heading back to the table. "She's single, but I don't know about any ex. We are just on a simple date, nothing more, and nothing less." Rushing he continued, "I have to go because she is on her way back."

Mark tried to say something but Harold hung up on him.

Maria saw him on the phone and as she reached the table and he hung up her eyebrows arched. "So who was that?"

Harold fumbled with the phone placing it back in his pants pocket. "Oh, oh that was my friend Mark. We have been friends since we were kids. He's just being nosey wanting to know how the date is going."

"Oh! That's nice to have a good friend like that. It's hard to find friends these days. Or keep them for that matter, there is always something going on. Jealousy or people just being fake."

Harold looked at her in the face. "You're right. I used to be jealous of Mark because he is good looking, cool and has always had his way with the ladies. I on the other hand was married, faithful, unhappy, and lonely because my ex wife was never around." At that moment thoughts of him having sex with Linda in the back of the bagel shop earlier popped in his head. He smiled but then caught himself straightening up.

"What's so funny Harold?"

"Nothing actually, I was just thinking about the bright side of it. And that's that it's all over because I'm happily divorced."

Maria went on, "I was never married but I had a live in boyfriend for five years. I thought we would eventually get married. But he would never get it together; he would go from job to job. Keep one for about six months and then be out of work for a few months. This went on for the last two years of the relationship. He grew up in this neighborhood that's how I moved out here because I'm originally from Long Island. Being that I'm not from out here, I knew very little people while he knew everyone. And this included the ladies who would always go out of their way to say hi to him whenever we were together. At first I thought it was nothing but then this one girl kept giving me dirty looks." She sucked her teeth and exhaled. "I saw her one day by herself and approached her and she told me Hector was messing around with her sister and had been for over three years now." Her eyes began to water lightly. "I realized something was going on because during the last six months of us being together there was a few times where he did not come home at night." She placed both palms in the air. "I thought maybe he was getting tired of me nagging him about getting and keeping a job." The waiter came over with a food cart and began filling the table up with all types of dishes and within seconds he was gone again.

"Well, anyway she set it so that I could actually see him and her sister together. And boy it was such a hurtful experience to watch Hector hand in hand with this other woman. Five years of my life had been thrown out the window. Surprisingly I didn't cry. Instead I ran home, packed all his stuff in plastic bags, and dragged them to the elevator and out the front of the building." She began to laugh. "I pulled no punches leaving him a note on each bag letting him know that I knew how low-down he was and that she could have him and all his drama."

Harold clumsily grabbed a fork and knife trying to cut into the juicy teriyaki breast.

He asked, "Did he ever come back."

"From time to time I see him on the street. At first he tried to talk to me, but I'd just walk past without saying a word so he'd stop. He once screamed that I'd always be his. He's from Honduras, that's how men are in those countries. They can cheat and do whatever, and the woman has to accept it." She began to arrange her dishes in front of her. "But I was born and raised here in New York so that's not me at all." Pausing momentarily she went on. "I saw him one day standing across the street from my building. A neighbor had called me and told me so I looked out the window. He looked as if he was drunk. I didn't go outside that day because I know that when he drinks he has a bad temper. When we first started dating I saw him beat a few guys up real bad by himself when he had a few drinks in him. He grew up in the streets, so he's tough. The fact that he was so sweet and tough made me attracted to him because I felt protected." She looked across the restaurant. "But now at times it's scary because the building I live in does not have security. The front door locks and has a buzzer but sometimes people leave it open. Everyone knows him in the building. The neighbors on my floor know we are not together. But someone else could always let him in."

"That sounds stressful," Harold said.

"Maybe I'm just being too worried. It's been four months and he hasn't done anything that drastic. I plan to move in a few months to the Bronx anyway. I'll be free then."

Harold was listening but gobbling down the food at the same time. It was delicious and he savored every bite. He even made faces with each swallow. Downing a fork full of rice, he drank some water beating on his chest to bring it down.

"If you feel like this maybe you should get an order of protection or something." Staring down at the empty mound of rice and small piece of chicken breast left he went on "I mean you have no one staying with you. Just to be on the safe side and make sure the authorities know that you have some concern about your safety you should file some paperwork."

In between bites she said, "I know. But right now let's just eat. I noticed you making faces so I assume the food must be that good, huh."

Harold's face lit up. "Maria, this food is so good!" He exhaled holding his belly "Wooo! I'm so full I cannot eat another bite."

"I'm good to, so let's get out of here."

Harold waved the waiter over to bring the check. A few minutes later the scrawny little man was back placing the receipt face down in front of Harold.

Maria gestured reaching into her pocketbook. "I'll pay half the bill."

Harold shook his head as to say no, snatched up the receipt, got up and started walking towards the cashier's desk.

Once outside Maria patted Harold upon the back. "Thanks for the lunch. Why don't we go back to my place have a drink and relax a bit? I just want to take off my shoes and kick back." She started to laugh. "That's kind of hard to do in a public place."

Harold agreed and they headed back to her place.

As they drove Maria mentioned. "You can park in a lot the next block over from my apartment." She pointed ahead. "You see where that bus went turn there, and then it will be on the left." Harold followed the bus and saw the lot just around the corner. A few moments later the car was parked and they were on their way.

Walking around the block Maria kept looking back and fourth nervously. It made Harold a bit edgy and he asked her if she was ok.

"I saw Hector's brother, and usually Hector is always somewhere around whenever I see his brother."

The heat was beating upon them both, and Harold felt a trickle of sweat rush down his armpit to his right wrist. Then they heard someone scream out.

"Maria!"

They both turned to see Hector's brother. When they turned back around Hector and another guy stood before them.

With beady eyes Hector looked at Maria. "Maria what are you doing? Didn't I tell you that you would always belong to me."

"Hector go away, please just go away. We're finished!"

Hector went to reach for Maria but Harold stepped in and nudged him. Hector looked at him with surprise. Harold was even surprised himself that he had the courage to do that. Hector's friend sucker punched him in the face knocking him to the ground. Maria started screaming as Hector and his friend started to punch and kick Harold repeatedly. He tried to get up but was kicked in the face, so he went back down covering his face balling into a fetus.

Maria screamed, "Stop! Stop· Hector! Leave him alone!"

She screamed for someone to call the police.

Once she realized that they were not going to stop beating Harold she jumped on Hector's back, scratching his face as she wrapped both arms around his neck. He became infuriated and flung her off him. She fell to the concrete and he rushed over smacking her twice in the face, swelling her lip. At the site of a man hitting a woman people started to rush over to the mayhem.

Hector called out to his friend, "Amigo! Let's go before the policia come!"

They both began to run, and in the process bumped past and knocked over a few people in the way.

Harold screamed holding his bloody and bruised face. He was kicking and rocking back and fourth. Maria ran over to him, kneeling over him with some napkins "Thank you Harold! I'm so, so sorry. I'm sorry! I did not think he was this crazy!"

Police sirens started blazing. Harold could hear walkie-talkies in the distance and approaching along with hard footsteps.

An officer yelled, "Move out the way! Move out the way!"

A hole opened between the onlookers and an officer came stumbling through. He tripped and lost his footing falling near Harold and Maria. The crowd started laughing. But the other officers started reaching for their guns thinking someone had pushed him to the ground.

He jumped up screaming to the other officers, "I fell, I'm fine!"

As if nothing happened the fallen officer kneeled down next to Maria who was wiping blood from Harold's face. Right away he noticed the handprint upon her face and how her hair sat disheveled.

He asked her, "Miss what happened? Do you both need medical attention? Does he have ID?"

Harold moaned and nodded.

She began crying, but still attended to Harold. "I'm ok, but he's going to need to be taken to the hospital. My ex-boyfriend and his friend jumped him. I tried to stop him and then he jumped on me too."

One officer called for an ambulance and another took their statement.

"Can you give a description of what they were wearing? And how they look?"

"He's wearing blue jeans, beige construction boots and a black tank top. He's Hispanic, 5'8, slim and has shoulder length black hair and black eyes. His friend is a little taller than him, Hispanic also but I did not get a good look at what he was wearing because it happened so quickly."

The ambulance arrived and the attendants were upon them placing Harold on the stretcher.

One of them asked, "Does he have ID?"

Maria responded between sobs. "Yes, he does."

The police officer grabbed her arm. "Go with them, we can finish the questions at the hospital. Do you know where the suspect lives?"

"No but I know his girlfriend lives in an apartment complex on 129th."

Maria got in the back of the ambulance while the officer radioed in the suspects' descriptions and possible location.

Maria cried. "Forgive me Harold! Forgive me. Please forgive me!"

Harold felt dizzy but he did remember Mark's words to him on the phone about being careful with jealous, crazy ex-boyfriends and husbands. When he came to again he was in the hospital. He had a chipped front tooth, and a cut just under the right eyebrow, which took four stitches.

Maria sat in the chair next to the bed and when the nurses finished and the doctor came in he asked her, "Are you his girlfriend?"

She smiled. "No, I'm just a friend. I witnessed what happened."

The doctor then turned to Harold. "Sir, we request that you stay overnight. We've taken x-rays of your head but we want to be sure you do not have any bone fractures, which we did not detect. But it does seem you have a minor concussion."

He started writing down some notes, staring periodically at Harold and then back to the clipboard. "You were very lucky that nothing is broke. Is there anyone you would like for us to contact, friends or relatives so they know of your whereabouts?"

Harold's face was aching and he moaned before saying, "Yes please call this number and let them know I'm here."

He gave the doctor a piece of paper.

The doctor looked at the piece of paper and stated, "I'll have the nurse do this right away for you. Rest up everything looks fine. If there is anything you need just ring for a nurse. You'll be out of here first thing tomorrow morning at ten a.m. as long as the x-rays come back showing no problems."

The doctor smiled at Maria and walked out.

Harold laid back and closed his eyes. Maria held his right hand "Harold if you don't mind I'm going to stay the night. I'll sleep in the chair."

Harold moaned. "Maria you don't have to do that. Go home to your bed and get some sleep. We've both had a very rough day. Don't feel—"

Before Harold could utter another word the officer from the scene came in.

"We've apprehended some subjects and we'd like you to come down to the station and review a line up."

Maria turned toward Harold. "I will be here in the morning to pick you up."

Harold moaned and stretched. "Ok."

Marks words about how the break up with Linda and then Jenny were getting the best of him resounded in his ear. He heard Marks voice in his mind as clear as the words through the phone receiver.

Chapter Twenty-Three

DEBRA AND LINDA had been fighting all day in the bagel shop. This time there were no fists, or slaps thrown. It was just a day full of arguments and name calling. By the time five o'clock rolled around they were exhausted. Linda's face was still beat red. Debra wore a scowl, which even the customers noticed. Some of the regulars asked her if she was ok. She was so furious that she held no punches back with letting them know she was not happy to be working with her bosses ex wife.

The phone rang and Debra picked up.

"Harry's Bagels."

Linda moved closer to Debra as to listen to the person on the other end.

Debra screamed, "Nurse from where? What! What happened! Are you sure he's ok? What hospital?"

Linda became frozen as she listened to Debra's conversation.

"He's being released tomorrow. So can he receive visits this evening?" She looked at Linda. "Okay, thank you nurse."

Debra hung up the phone and grabbed the wall. Tears began to fall down her face. Linda heard the phone conversation but did not know whom they were talking about she tried to pretend she didn't care until a customer asked Debra what happened and she mentioned Harold had gotten into a scuffle with two men and was in the hospital, then she almost collapsed to the floor.

Linda screamed, "We have to close the shop and go to the hospital." She looked around at all the customers and yelled, "Everyone we are closing right now!"

Her and Debra served all the customers, locked the door, cleaned up and closed the shop all within twenty-five minutes. And they managed to do it without arguing. In fact they acted as if the fight earlier never happened at all.

They checked in at the emergency desk and got Harold's room number. On the elevator the silence between them both was creepy because they both never stayed quiet for more than a few minutes at a time without talking.

When they entered Harold's room and caught sight of him laid up in the bed, face all bruised tears began to swell up in both of their eyes. He heard them enter and stared toward them both briefly before closing his eyes again.

Debra held his hand. "Harold what happened?"

He jerked and moaned a bit before saying, "They got the best of me. Maria's ex-boyfriend and his friend. They surrounded us as I walked her to her building." He started to laugh, squinting because the stitches above his eyebrows were bothering him. "I should have listened to Mark and stayed away. He warned me about pretty ladies with jealous ex-boyfriends and husbands." He shook his head. "I wouldn't listen."

Linda and Debra chuckled. Harold joined in, but also moaned a little.

Debra mentioned, "Speaking of Mark, I'm going to call him because I'm sure he would like to know where you're at."

Harold leaned forward and then lay back quickly. "Don't do that because I don't want to have to admit to him he was right."

"Harold just keep quiet because I'm calling him now." Debra started to dial Mark's number.

"Nina hi, its Debra from the bagel shop, Harold has been in an accident. Is Mark there?"

Debra kept her eyes on Harold while she talked. "Yes! He's ok. I just got here. He had a fight and they are holding him overnight at the hospital."

Debra could hear Nina telling Mark that Harold's in the hospital. She was excited and was speaking a hundred words a minute. She finally put Mark on the phone.

"Hi Mark. He's at Holliswood Hospital and can get visits up to nine-thirty p.m."

"We're on our way. Is Linda there with you?"

Calmly Debra replies, "Yes she is."

Mark hung up the phone telling Nina to put some shoes on because they were going to the hospital.

***

Mouhab and Jenny rode around Central Park in the back of the horse and buggy. They laughed and talked about everything from fashion to finances and Jenny was very impressed with Mouhab's knowledge.

As the ride came to an end Mouhab helped Jenny off the buggy. They walked side by side. Abruptly he stopped walking and stood in front of her. "Jenny what is a beautiful woman like yourself doing without a boyfriend?"

Jenny smiled shaking her head. "Mouhab, it's a very long story. And I'm not sure you have the time to listen to it all." She stopped and looked into his black pearly eyes.

He smiled. "Why don't you try me? Let's sit over here on the bench."

She exhaled with a smile and followed him to the bench.

"Okay, I'm listening," he said with a smile.

"Well, I just went through a break up before the trip to Egypt. I thought he was the perfect match for me. He was kind, considerate and he made me feel very special. He told me he was divorced, but his wife showed up at my door one day with a child telling me he was cheating on her and that he wanted to leave her with the child."

Mouhab asked, "Jenny do you know for sure that's the case. Or even if that's his wife?"

Jenny ran her hands through her hair. "Well, when I told him about it he tried to deny it. He kept insisting that he was divorced and that his ex-wife was just not happy that he was doing well without her." She started to laugh. "Mouhab why do you care anyway?"

Mouhab stared into her eyes. "I ask because I care about your well being. Sometimes it's as if you're thinking about something else although you may be in the middle of having a conversation or doing something. And now I know what it is; it seems to me as if you are unsure about everything that happened between you and him. Your day is consumed by reliving the past."

Jenny yelled slapping his hand. "Mouhab what are you a psychic or something. You're scaring me."

Mouhab got up. "Let's walk back, the nights are so beautiful. New York is a wonderful place."

Jenny smiled, grabbing his hand. "Yes New York is the greatest city in the world."

They walked hand in hand the full ten blocks to her place taking in the scenery of the busy streets. Couples walked, cars passed, taxis stopped for passengers. Occasionally they'd see a homeless person huddled next to a building sleeping with a blanket.

Once inside the apartment Jenny walked him over into the bedroom where they made love passionately. Mouhab could not help but to wonder if she gave herself to him or to the love she lost but still longs for.

Jenny stayed up for hours that night. Her eyes were full of tears and she sniffed a little although she tried her best to hide her sorrow. Mouhab pretended to be asleep, but he heard her cries and felt her pain as if it was his own. He was saddened by the reality that her heart belonged to another man.

Chapter Twenty-Four

WHEN THE HOSPITAL discharged Harold, Maria was not there but the officer from the scene was there. The young cop shook Harold's hand and introduced himself.

"Sir, we apprehended the two men who assaulted you yesterday and we'd like you to come down and fill out some paperwork. Maria identified the men as being her ex-boyfriend and a friend of his."

"Okay," Harold responded.

"When you get there just ask the desk sergeant for Officer Ramos."

Harold just nodded and waited to be discharged. After he signed the release papers at the nurses' station he was free to go. He walked out the doors and right away and jumped in a cab.

"Here's where I need to go." Harold handed him the parking ticket from the lot before laying his head on the seat and closing his eyes.

The cabby asked, "Are you ok sir?"

"Yeah, I'm ok. I'm just a bit tired. They have me on some antibiotic and the meds have me a little sluggish that's all, I'm fine."

Harold briefly opened his eyes to look at the old white guy who wore his head shaved like Kojak donning black shades.

"He's one cool, old cat," Harold thought to himself.

The first thing Harold did when he got home was call the bagel shop. He was relieved when Debra picked up.

"How is everything Deb?"

Debra huffed. "Linda didn't come in because Jonathon is sick."

Harold immediately got upset. "Aaaaah man! I can't win for losing Deb. When it rains it pours. Is it really busy today?"

Debra was going crazy because the place had stayed packed since early morning. But she did not want him to worry so she replied, "It's nothing that I can't handle."

"I know Deb I just don't want you by yourself that's all." Pausing a moment he said, "I'm going to come in around two o' clock."

Debra protested, "Wait until tomorrow Harold. Get your rest I'll be fine."

"Nope I'll be in today. And make sure you call Linda to make sure she is all right. I know you two have not been the best of friends. But it's times like these that people need to know that they have someone in their corner. And you're a woman so I'm sure you can relate to what she is going through right now."

"You're right. I already told her I would stop by after work to see if I can do something for her and Jonathan. Maybe I'll cook them dinner."

"That's my girl." Harold hung up the phone.

Chapter Twenty-Five

MOUHAB AWOKE AT 9 a.m. so by the time the mail arrived at 10:45 he was about on his way out the door. He opened the door to find the mailman sorting Jenny's mail.

"Good morning sir. Should I give you the mail?"

"Good morning to you as well. Yes, I'll take it and give it to the young lady."

The mailman handed Mouhab a handful of envelopes and walked off to the next door. Jenny was asleep and Mouhab did not want to awake her so he placed the mail on the kitchen table. Before leaving he scribbled a note asking her to call him later to set up a time for dinner.

Jenny woke around noon and she slid her foot over to the left side of the bed, but Mouhab's was not there.

She slid out of bed and washed up before walking into the kitchen and finding the note Mouhab had left.

"Mouhab," she said softly running her hands through her hair. Sorting through the bills she found a letter from Nina and Mark. She remembered them immediately as being friends of Harold's. She ripped open the envelope and found a card, which had a small note, tucked inside.

Dear: Jenny,

This is Nina, Marks fiancée. I would like to invite you to our wedding on August 20th. The location and time is on the invitation card. I know I should mind my own business but Harold as you know is Mark's best friend. Harold really is a good guy Jenny. Linda lied to you when she told you all those bad things. He is not still married to her, and her son is not his."

Jenny dropped the letter to the table, she felt as if she was having an anxiety attack. Catching her breath she sat down placed her hands up to her forehead and began crying. She picked up the letter again and continued to read from where she left off.

He misses you so much. You are the best thing that has happened to him in a long while. You two make such a good couple. Even Mark thinks you are the right one for him.

I hope to see you at our wedding

Love,

Nina and Mark

Jenny read the invitation and realized the wedding was in two days and she wasn't going to miss it for the world. She just hoped that Harold would show up. She was also looking forward to seeing Linda and settling the score with her for messing things up.

She looked again at the table and saw the brief note by Mouhab. A feeling of guilt came over as she thought about how nice and understanding Mouhab had been.

She was snapped out of her daze by the sound of water hitting the floor. Right then she realized the bathtub was overflowing. She ran into the bathroom shutting off the faucet and laughed at herself because she would have fell on her butt had it not been for her grabbing onto the door handle.

After mopping up the water and drying the floor up with towels Jenny got in the tub, squirted some bubble bath in the water and laid back allowing her head to rest above the water.

She whispered, "It feels soooo good."

Harold walked through the front door of the bagel shop and the regulars started greeting him. He laughed, bowed and then almost tripped as he walked behind the counter. Debra stopped what she was doing, walked over to him and hugged him.

"I'm glad you're all right Harold. I was scared for a minute." She smiled. "You're like a brother to me so you better be careful."

Harold playfully rubbed Debra's head. "They got me pretty good, but I'm all right. I was supposed to go down to the precinct at two but I called and told them I'd make it down there tomorrow to fill out the paperwork." Harold smirked. "They found the two guys." Maria identified her ex-boyfriend in a line-up.

Debra asked, "Are you going to see her again?"

Harold shrugged his shoulders. "Who knows? She said she would be at the hospital this morning, but she didn't show. Maybe she's embarrassed by everything." Harold began fixing a customers order.

"Tuna on whole wheat?" he asked just to make sure.

The customer replied, "You know the deal Harold."

Harold turned toward Debra; "I think I had enough with *Love.com* and all it offers. I almost got myself killed with this fixer upper that's for sure."

Debra began to laugh. "Try the phone chat line."

Harold shook his head. "That's all I need is to try to hook up without seeing a picture. With my luck I'll meet a sumo wrestler named Sally with a high pitch woman's voice."

All the customers began laughing at Harold's remark. Debra began laughing hysterically.

The day went by quickly and before Debra or Harold realized it was about time to close. Harold swept and mopped the floor while Debra started to gather all the dishes in the dishwasher. The front doors buzzer chimed and a masked man came in brandishing a revolver. Harold didn't notice because he was mopping with his back turned toward the door. The masked man was right on top of him by the time he turned around.

"Put your hands up or I'll shoot you. Don't look at me."

Harold dropped the mop to the floor putting both hands up above the shoulders.

"Hurry up, let's go to the register. And don't look at me or I'll shoot you."

Harold was stuck and could not move. But the masked man pointed the gun in his face, grabbed him by the front of the shirt and dragged him to the register. "Open it! And I mean now!"

Harold fidgeted pressing the registers keys.

The drawer opened and the masked man clumsily snatched all the money out. He shoved Harold to the floor and ran out the front door.

As soon as the robber left Debra came from the back.

She ran to Harold. "Are you ok Harold? I saw him; I was peaking through the door and saw him pointing the gun at you. I'm glad you listened because I was scared he was going to shoot."

Harold still sat in the corner. He was shaking and beads of sweat formed across his forehead. He finally found his voice and told Debra to call the police.

"I'm ok just hurry-hurry and call the police!"

Debra quickly called 911 and went back to comfort Harold who had now gotten out the corner and was leaning over the customer counter with his hands to his face.

Harold kept his hands up to his head. Debra watched him until the police arrived. Four officers came through the door and the first officer asked Harold if he needed any medical attention. Harold told them no and Debra filled out the report and gave a description of the robber. Debra told the officer there was something familiar about

the robber but she could not put a finger on it. He handed
her a card, telling her if she remembered or came across
anything else to call him immediately.

They closed the shop while the police officers
watched. Harold drove home in a daze, but nevertheless
he managed to get there without incident.

On the way to Linda's, Debra tried to recollect where
she heard that voice. The robber's voice sounded so
familiar. His body image she saw somewhere as well.
Finally she gave up and just thought about how Harold
was taking it. First he gets beat up by two men and then
he gets robbed with a gun placed to his head.

The cab pulled in front of Linda's building; Debra
paid the fee and got out. She buzzed Linda's apartment
and Linda answered right away.

"Is that you Debra?"

"It's me."

"Take the elevator to the second floor, get out and it's
the second door to the right. I'll be waiting to let you in."

Debra stepped out the elevator and walked to the right
and knocked on the second door.

"It's just me and Jonathan because Carl went out to
the bar about two hours ago."

The name Carl resonated within Debra's head but she
paid it no attention.

"Go sit down," she told Linda. Looking around she
continued, "I'm going to fix you and Jonathan dinner. I'll
find my way in the kitchen and if I need you for anything
I'll holler."

Debra fixed some steak, wild rice and corn. Jonathan was still feeling sick and ate very little before going to his room. Her and Linda devoured the food as if it was their first meal of the day.

Linda licked her lips. "Man that was good. It feels so good to finally be able to sit down and enjoy a meal and not worry about having to cook it."

"I know exactly what you mean Linda; I was married for ten years before I got divorced. All that fool wanted me to do was stay home and serve him on hand and foot."

Linda looked toward Debra and said, "Debra I had it made with Harold. But the fact is I fell out of love with Harold a long time ago. I lust for him now and then, but I don't love him. It's sick but I get jealous when I know he's with someone else, although I know they may be better for him then me."

Debra stared into her eyes and saw the woman's sincerity. "At least you can be honest about it."

At that moment the door came crashing down.

Both of them jumped up screaming.

Armored police wearing black uniforms stormed the apartment. They rushed the two ladies making them sit on the couch and place their hands behind their backs.

One of the officers asked, "Ma'am, where is your son?"

The man's tone reflected more of a statement then a question.

"His rooms in the back. The last door to the right."

The officer walked back there while the others began searching the apartment. A minute later he was back in the room with Jonathan who ran to Linda's arms.

Debra asked. "What's going on? Why are you here?"

A plain-clothes detective asked Debra, "Is this your apartment?"

"No! This is hers. But I'm her friend. What's the problem?"

The detective handed Linda a pack of papers. "We have a warrant to search the premises. Your husband Carl Freely was arrested for robbery."

Linda dropped her head and began sobbing.

Jonathan was in her lap and called out to her. "Mommy, mommy."

Debra was in shock but reality was beginning to hit her. She realized that Carl was the one who robbed the bagel shop. The voice, the tall image, both of these she had come across before.

An officer called out to the detective from one of the back rooms. "Sir, we have something."

The detective left and came back up front with two revolvers and one semi-automatic handgun in a plastic evidence bag. He looked at Linda. "We are also going to need you to come down to the station for questioning."

Linda was sobbing uncontrollably. "I haven't done anything wrong. Why should I be put through this? I have a child. Who's going to watch Jonathan?"

"We can take him to a relative; the both of you can ride in a squad car to where you have to go drop him off.

Or they can come to the precinct and get him. Which ever is easiest for you." He didn't bother to wait for a reply he walked to the back where the other officers were still searching.

Debra watched on with disbelief. The only thing she was sure about was that Carl was the same person who robbed the store the first and second time. It was just too much of a coincidence for him to not have done both.

Two more detectives walked through where the front door of the apartment would have been had it not gotten blown off the hinges. Neither of them said anything to the ladies they walked to the back and could be heard talking with the other detective.

The first detective came back and walked over to Linda and began reading her Miranda rights.

Debra became hysterical. "What is she under arrest for?"

"Her husband Carl signed a sworn statement stating she planned the first robbery a few months back of the bagel shop."

Linda held her head down and didn't look up.

Debra asked, "Is this true Linda?"

Linda whispered, "I'm sorry, I'm so sorry." She finally looked toward Debra. "My mother's number is on the fridge, please call her and tell her to come get Jonathan."

Jonathan began screaming at the top of his lungs while Debra tried to calm him down. He tried to run out into the hallway behind Linda but Debra grabbed him.

He kicked away in her arms and even tried to bight her but Debra held him tightly. At this point she began to cry herself. She held Jonathan close to her and they cried together. Debra cried for them both, but more so for the little boy who would forever be scarred by the image of seeing his mother carried away in handcuffs.

A little while later Harold showed up.

"What's this?" Harold asked in disbelief. He walked through the doorway with both hands held to the top of his head.

Debra looked at him with pity. "I'm so sorry Harold."

"They called me saying they have Carl in custody and he admitted to the robberies. This one and the one a few months back."

Debra was still holding Jonathan. "I don't know if Linda was in on this one. But apparently she was in on the first one because they just arrested her after Carl signed a sworn statement."

Harold sat on the couch in disbelief. He didn't even notice Linda's mother when she came to get Jonathan. She walked out with her grandson without saying a word to anyone.

Debra grabbed Harold by both hands. "Let's go home Harold. There is nothing we can do here."

The police were still conducting their search as they walked out the doorway together down the hall toward the elevator.

Harold looked toward Debra. "You know Deb, today was the first day I prayed to God in about a year. I have so much to be grateful for and I never take the time out to thank him for the blessings he's thrown my way." He put his arm around her shoulder "Today I faced death twice and won. And I thank God for it."

Debra smiled. "Harold God is definitely in your corner."

Chapter Twenty-Six

THE DAY WAS bright; a slight breeze accompanied the warm weather.

Jenny and Mouhab walked from one end of the block and back to where they started. "Jenny lets go to the mart and do some shopping. I would like to buy you something."

Jenny's mind was very heavy. "Mouhab I need to talk to you about something very important."

He looked toward her then back to the busy streets. "Lets go shopping and then you can tell me what you have to tell me. Right now let's enjoy the day, ok."

Jenny was becoming impatient. "Ok, Mouhab but we need to talk."

Mouhab knew deep inside what Jenny wanted to talk to him about, but for now he would enjoy as much of her company as he could.

Walking past a fruit shop Mouhab pulled at Jenny for her to follow him inside. The Chinese couple behind the counter smiled at them both. Mouhab grabbed a basket and began grabbing pears, apples, and oranges and when he came to the strawberries he plucked some out their basket and fed one to Jenny. He decided that since today was probably their last day together he would make the day memorable. He wanted her to remember him for having a gentle heart.

He walked to the counter with the fruit and she followed closely. After he paid she grabbed one of the bags and walked out the door. He got his change, toying with the coins for a moment before placing them in his pocket. The Chinese woman smiled and he smiled back

Mouhab huffed then sucked his teeth before chewing into a pear. "Jenny let's walk and talk. Tell me all there is that my heart dreads to hear."

Jenny looked toward the ground as she walked. "Mouhab, I found out the truth. My heart told me so but I was relying on my thoughts of most men in general as being liars and cheaters."

Mouhab replied, "Huuh."

Jenny got quiet and then continued "I found out that he's not still married and that the boy by his ex wife isn't his. She lied so that we would not be together." She held her free hand up to her mouth "Now I feel like such a fool because I did not believe him when he tried to tell me she was lying. I wanted to believe him but I just couldn't bring myself to."

Mouhab stopped walking. He stood in front of Jenny. But she did not look at him "So what are you going to do Jenny." Softly he said, "Look at me. What are you going to do?"

She looked into his eyes, up into the deep pools of blackness "I was invited to his best friends wedding, which is tomorrow. They sent me an invitation, telling me the whole story. So I will go and try to work things out. That's if he still wants me."

Mouhab smirked and his black eyes held a tint of water within them. "Of course he will want you. What man wouldn't want a woman like you?"

Jenny grabbed Mouhab by the arm. "Mouhab, I'm so sorry. You've been such a gentleman but I have to follow my heart or else I'll hate myself and always wonder what if?"

"I know Jenny. I know that your heart belongs to another man." He placed both hands upon the sides of her face, "There is nothing either one of us can do about the matters of the heart. We can only go with the beat. I will miss you, believe me I will miss you always. I will leave the states beaten and defeated, but I will be truly happy for you and rejoice in the creators blessings that he has allowed you to see beyond your emotions which have blinded you causing to almost lose that which you've found covenant in. Love is a place of refuge and comfort."

Mouhab kissed Jenny for the last time upon her cheek, hugged her tightly and then walked off. She called out to him but he did not turn back. She watched him walk block after block but he never turned back once. Once he was out of distance she fell against the wall of the building and began sobbing uncontrollably. She fell to the pavement, sitting resting her back against the wall. She cried, cried and cried until the sun began to burn her skin. She didn't love Mouhab but she cared for him. She cared for him enough not to want him to hurt. She wanted to call him but quickly decided against it.

Her crimes of the heart were to end here right now. She would cry all the tears out of her she could and leave Mouhab in the past. Her heart and love belonged to another and even if he did not want it she needed to free Mouhab from her. She would never care for him the way he did her, for true love only strikes once in a lifetime.

Chapter Twenty-Seven

THE DAY OF Nina and Mark's wedding Mark was getting cold feet and if it were not for Harold he probably would have disappeared. Harold kept his friend in-line by telling him he was doing the right thing.

Harold patted Mark on his back. "Mark, I'm proud of you. You've matured a lot. Now it's like you're the one with all the answers. You have a great woman in Nina. You two are gonna be very happy together, watch and see."

Mark looked worried and his face was sweaty. "Harold you know me this is the biggest step I've ever taken in my life. Getting married at one time was my worst nightmare. Now I'm here, and I'm scared as hell to tell you the truth." He started to laugh, "I'm about to crap in my pants."

Harold started to laugh. "Don't do that now. You'll stink up the whole church. Remember how you used to fart when we were kids and stink up Mrs. Black classroom?"

Mark started to laugh uncontrollably. His face turned beet red. "Yeah, she would send me to the nurse every time."

"It was so bad that I almost threw up one time smelling it."

Mark hugged Harold. "You're the best. I feel better after getting that laugh in. It took the jitters right out of me." He struck a muscle man pose. "I'm ready to see Nina and make her my bride."

"That's what I'm talking about," Harold told his friend as he fixed Mark's tie.

Just then David walked in. "What's up guys?" He shook Harold's hand and quickly reached up and messed up his tie.

"When are you gonna change David? You're always going to be the prankster huh."

David replied. "Yup!" and then started laughing again.

Harold shook his head.

"So are you ready for the big day big guy?" Dave asked Mark.

Mark replied, "I was a little nervous but Harold here set me straight." He patted Harold on the shoulder. "This guy is great!"

Mark's father knocked on the door then stuck his head in the room. "Five more minutes son." He disappeared back out the door.

"Whoa!" Mark exhaled.

Someone yelled, "Let's go champ!" Then all the guys started chanting in unison, "Let's go champ! Let's go champ!"

Everyone followed Mark into the chapel hallway. He walked to the front of the church while the rest of the groomsmen paired up with their bridesmaids. Harold was the best man and he was delighted to be handing over the ring to Mark to give to Nina.

The piano player began to play and one by one couple by couple began to step down the aisle toward the front making way for the flower girl was dropping petals along the aisle leading to the threshold. Pretty soon, the wedding march began to play and Nina made her way down the isle.

The reverend spoke. "We are here to gather this man and woman in holy matrimony. Will you Mark Johnson have Nina Pisa to be your wife? Will love her, comfort and keep her, and forsaking all other remain true to her as long as you both shall live?"

Mark smiled at Nina. "I will."

The reverend then turned to Nina "Will you, Nina Pisa, have Mark Johnson to be your husband? Will you love him, comfort and keep him, and forsaking all other remain true to him as long as you both shall live?"

Nina looked at the reverend and then Mark "I will."

The reverend asked for the ring. Harold slipped Mark his ring and smiled as he watched him slip it on Nina's petite finger.

The reverend smiled widely. "You may now kiss the bride."

Mark grabbed Nina and they kissed like their love was meant to last forever.

Everyone started cheering, clapping and whistling. Mark turned toward Harold and they hugged one another. Nina came over hugged him kissing him on the cheek.

"Let's go outside and take pictures," Nina yelled.

As they got outside the church doors parked right in front were four limos. Mark tapped Harold on his shoulder asking, "Harold can you get the camera out that limo?"

"Sure."

Harold walked over to the limo opening the door. He jumped back startled. He almost tripped over his feet. Jenny got out wearing a beautiful white wedding gown.

She ran to him and threw her arms around him. "I love you Harold and I always will."

Harold hugged her and tears started to stream down his face. He didn't know what to say.

Jenny hesitated at first, and then spoke. "Harold can I ask you something?"

"Of course!"

She got on one knee. "Will you marry me?"

Everyone started screaming.

Harold picked Jenny up and hugged her close to him. "Of course. I love you Jenny."

The reverend, Mark and Nina came down the church steps.

Jenny said excited. "Then let's do it now."

"Jenny we don't have any rings."

"Well, then we can get married without them. I just want to do it now. I don't want to wait and take the chance that it never happens. I lost you one time, but its not going to happen again!"

Jenny grabbed Harold's hand firmly. The reverend stepped in-between them both while everyone surrounded them in the churches parking lot.

"Will you Harold Fenly have Jenny Reston to be your wife? Will you love her, comfort and keep her, and forsaking all other and remain true to her as long as you both shall live?

Harold looked into Jenny's eyes. "I will."

The reverend tells Harold, "Repeat, I Harold Fenly take thee Jenny Reston to be my wife, and before God and these witnesses I promise to be a faithful and true husband."

Harold did as the reverend asked.

The reverend turns to Jenny.

"Will you Jenny Reston have Harold Fenly to be your husband? Will you love him, comfort and keep him, and forsaking all other remain true to him as long as you both shall live?"

Jenny smiles and says, "I will."

"Repeat, I Jenny Reston take thee Harold Fenly to be my husband, and before God and these witnesses I promise to be a faithful and true wife."

With a huge smile, she does as she's asked.

Someone in the crowd yells out, "You may now kiss the bride!"

Everyone starts to laugh. The pastor laughs and repeats, "You may now kiss the bride."

Harold and Jenny begin kissing. Mark and Nina hug them both and they all lock arms.

Cameras begin flashing one after the other and the party starts right in the parking lot. Someone brought out a boom box and people start dancing.

Jenny asked, "Where's Linda?"

"She is in jail with her husband."

"What?"

Jenny did not bother to ask why. She just got down with the train Nina, Mark and Harold started around the parking lot.

Chapter Twenty-Eight

LINDA LAY UPON the top bunk in the cell, which she shared with Rachel who was facing a twenty-five year to life sentence for killing her abusive husband. With a picture of Jonathan in her hand she hummed to herself. Being that Rachel was out on a visit Linda had the cell to herself so there was no need to be quiet. Rachel hated when Linda would hum, but Linda did it often because it's the only thing, which calmed her nerves besides looking at Jonathan and her husband Carl's pictures.

The C.O. called out, "Linda Freely on the visit."

Linda sat up and got off the bunk hurriedly. Sticking her head out the cell gateway she screamed, "I'm coming!"

She wondered who it was that had come to see her because the only visits she had been getting were from her mother, father and aunt who would come on the weekends. Linda was excited to be able to get out the cell and off the tier. One hour outside for recreation once a day was beginning to ware on her. The last four months had been devastating to the point where she really did not care about her personal appearance like she used to. Everyday she'd take a shower, towel dry, brush and put her hair up in a ponytail.

Today since she did not know who it was coming to see her she decided to wear her hair down. Hurriedly she unfastened the ponytail, looked in the mirror, began to brush and cursed at herself taking notice of all the split ends.

"Shit!"

She brushed some more and decided to just leave it be. The C.O. opened the tier gate for her. The officer on the tier told her smiling, "Have a great visit Mrs. Freely."

Once within the hallway Linda was escorted down in the elevator to the first floor. When Linda walked in the visiting room the first person she saw was Jenny who was looking more beautiful than ever. This she even had to admit to herself. She couldn't help but to stare at the younger woman for a few seconds feeling a ting of jealousy creep through her veins. Then she took notice of Harold who waved at her when their eyes locked upon one another. Linda walked over to the table and sat behind the glass divider. Her lips were closed tight, and she looked tired.

Harold was the first to speak. "It was so hard to bring myself to come here even after all this time. I really can't believe it came to this. You really surprised me. I could not believe it at first."

Harold began twitching, and fidgeting his fingers. He looked from Linda to Jenny. Jenny rubbed Harold's back trying not to make eye contact with Linda. She despised the woman and couldn't bring herself to look at her for two long without saying anything negative.

Linda held her forehead, tears started to fall. Her eyes met Harold's once again; she tried to reach his soul. Her eyes pleaded.

"Harold can we speak alone. Please! Please! I just need for you to understand."

Harold turned over to Jenny who looked away angrily. "Jenny I'll be out in no more than ten minutes."

Jenny got up and didn't look back. She walked over to the officer's station and he let her out. Both Harold and Linda watched her leave. Once she was through the gate Linda's gaze fell to the table.

Harold questioned, "Why? Why did you do it?"

Linda began crying again. "Harold, I'm so, so sorry. I don't know what I was thinking. I never wanted to see you hurt." She placed both hands upon the top of the divider. "Carl and I were doing badly, and with the baby and neither of us working the stress of it all took over. I never meant to hurt you."

Harold was agitated. "Linda all you had to do was ask me, I would have helped you." Fidgeting his fingers between one another he continued. "Things were over between us, but I never would want to see you doing badly. All you had to do was ask!"

"Harold! Harold I'm sorry! Please forgive me! You've always been a better person than me." Her voice tone became lower. "But I've changed. I've changed, you have to believe me."

Harold took inventory of her, thinking to himself how this was not the Linda he knew. How nothing about her was the same.

Harold calmed himself down placing both hands upon the divider. Linda placed her hands on top of his. They talked without saying words.

"Linda if you need anything just call us. We're here for you."

Linda wiped at her eyes. "Ok. Thank you!"

He got up, walked off and didn't look back.

As Linda watched him, her heart ached. She sucked her teeth, pounding her palms upon the table before getting up.

Jenny stood outside the jailhouse waiting for Harold. He walked over to her and they hugged and he almost stumbled with her as his right foot slid on a pebble.

Jenny started laughing. "My clumsy Harold." She kissed him. "But I love! I love you!"

Harold laughed. "Thanks to Love.com"

Jenny chuckled, kissing him again whispering into his ear "I love Love.com too."

They both looked back toward the jailhouse. Hand in hand they turned and walked off to the car.

Epilogue

SIX MONTHS AFTER the weddings, Harold, Jenny, Mark and Nina bought a house together out in Long Island. All were happily married and both Jenny and Nina were expecting. Harold and Mark were two of the happiest men alive.

Linda did three months in jail and was released after Harold pleaded on her behalf for the court to give her leniency because she had a son to take care of. The court also granted an order of protection against her stipulating that she could not come within 1000 feet of him or Jenny.

Carl was sentenced to a six-year sentence in prison for the robberies. He was mandated to take alcoholics anonymous and an alternative to violence program while in prison.

Mouhab still loved Jenny but he moved on and started dating a famous British model. From time to time he wondered how Jenny was doing.

LOVE IS A STRANGE THING!

Love Don't Live Here/ISBN: 0977100413

"Love Don't Live Here," the first book from a generational series. This is a story about two young African American women who become single mothers through different circumstances. The two women invite us into the world of relationships and single motherhood. In the end we all find out "it's about doing and being the best that one can be."

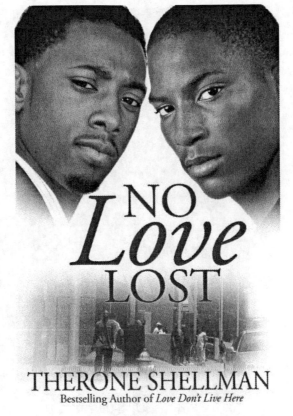

NO *Love* LOST

THERONE SHELLMAN
Bestselling Author of *Love Don't Live Here*

No Love Lost/ISBN: 0977100421

A novel about the realities young men face-coming of age and making decisions that affect everyone around them.

Although the novel is very real, gritty and filled with all the true to life elements of the street "by no means is this novel meant to glorify crime and violence." Instead it is a real look into the world so many of Americas young get lured into.

No Love lost is a story, which will entertain and educate

Even Numbers/ISBN:097710043X

Never in a million years had Dominga ever thought a man like James would look in her direction, let alone fall in love with her. With the responsibility of a five-year-old daughter, well frankly, she'd thought she would end up with some guy who felt sorry for her or someone who just knew she'd stick around because of her little girl. But James adores her and he's smart and successful and he makes good money. He's not the finest man she's ever been with; certainly not as fine as that loser ex-husband of hers, but then Olivia is crazy about him and everyone knows little girls need a daddy in their lives.

Who better than a fly on the wall, to tell this narrative tale? After all a fly would have the best seat in the house when it comes to spying on a family. And things aren't always, as they seem, particularly in this home. When Dominga met James she thought she'd be happy again and for quite awhile, she was. Then things got bad…really bad!

You see, James likes little girls; he *really* likes little girls. He goes out of his way to pacify and indulge Dominga in her every wish so that he can spend time alone with her precious little girl. He figures Dominga will never notice as long as she has all the things she's ever wanted. In fact, he counts on it. James loves Saturday mornings. That's when Dominga has her regular hair appointment and he is alone with Olivia. At night he's unable to get to her, because Dominga is at home; so he goes out into several different neighborhoods and lurks in the bars hoping to meet other needy women with little girls. And when he does, he worms his way into their homes armed with drinks, drugs and empty promises; knowing that once he takes care of mother's needs he'll be invited in. But he'll only stay long enough to get what he wants. These women think he wants *them*, but it's their little girls he's after. He can't wait to touch them, to smell them and to use their soft tender bodies and once he's finished with them, he disappears from their lives.

Dominga is in denial or maybe she really doesn't have a clue, but there is no stopping James. That is until someone steps in to make sure James would never again be able to destroy the lives of innocent women and their little girls.

Look for other upcoming titles to be released by Third Eye Publishing, Inc.

Visit
www.thirdeyepublishing.org